I0784586

This is a work of fiction. All of the characters, organizations, and events portrayed in this novel are either products of the author's imagination or are used fictitiously.

Cover photograph : ©Gemphotography | Dreamstime.com
Translation : Adrianna Hunter, that.adriana@gmail.com
Edition : Joanne Starer

Copyright © 2019, Highwire Publishing Inc.

ISBN 978-2-924263-18-1 (printed edition)
ISBN 978-2-924263-05-1 (ebook)

First Edition: September 2014

www.highwire-pub.com

The Predator

By Jane O'Neil

Translated by

Adriana Hunter

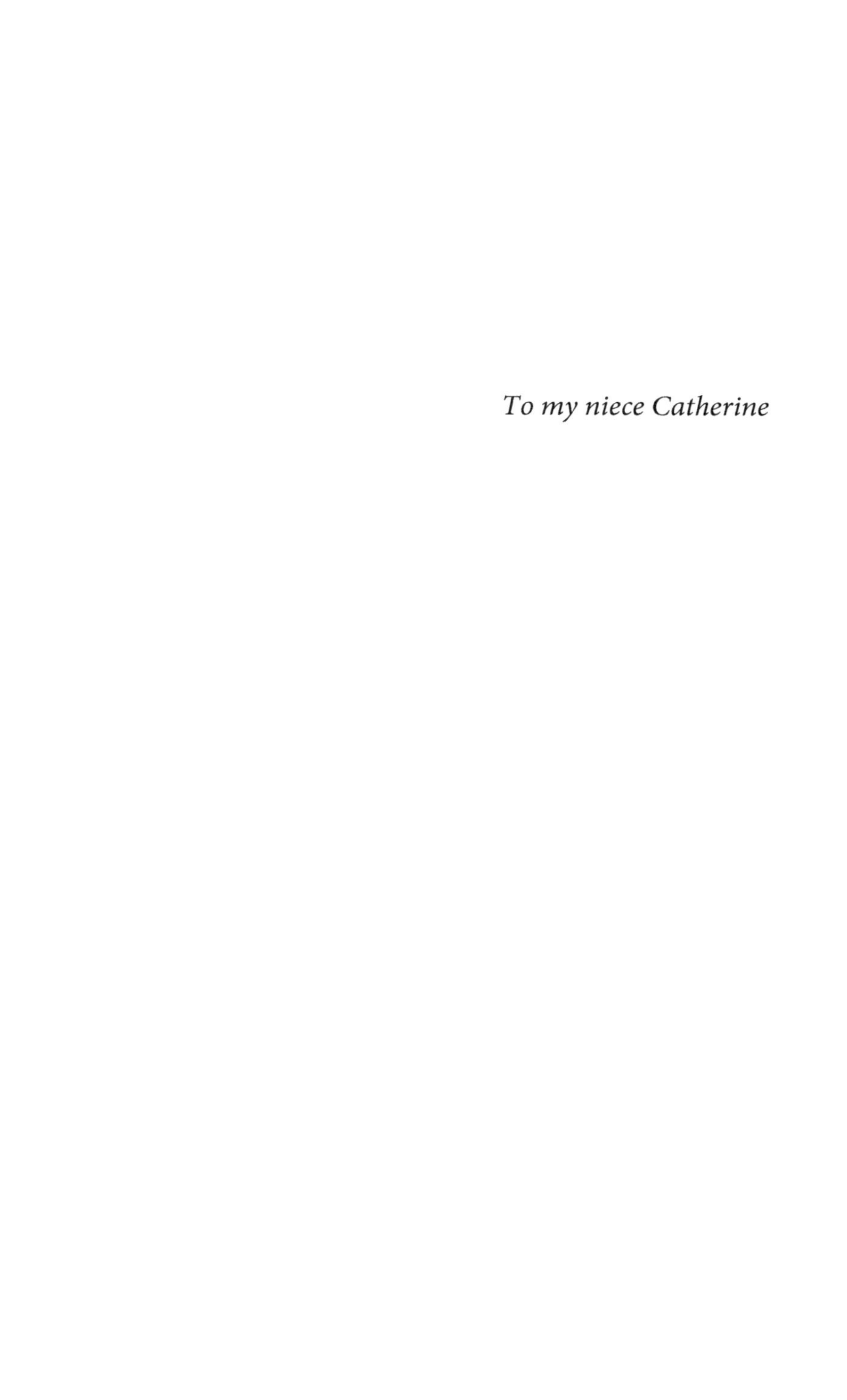

To my niece Catherine

1
Caught in the Trap

The little girl crouched in a corner of the cave, trying to keep her terror under control. But it wasn't exactly easy keeping calm with these shivers running up and down her slight frame. If she could just bring her arms up around her shoulders, she might be able to warm up. But her kidnapper had taken the precaution of tying her hands.

Working with unusual focus for a child her age, she tried to untie the knot restraining her hands behind her back. She fingered the rope, searching for loops she might be able to loosen and free her hands. However, as much as she pulled, the knots were well secured and wouldn't give in. After several minutes of dogged concentration, she lost patience and kicked violently at the rope tethering her to a metal ring on the ground. This outburst of frustration only served to tighten the ties. Feeling discouraged and helpless, she started to cry quietly; and then, unable to hold back her fear any longer, she broke down into sobs of despair.

"Stop sniveling," snarled a deep, menacing voice from the mouth of the cave.

Startled, the little girl stopped abruptly and froze. He wasn't going to start tormenting her again, was he? It had been nearly a whole day since he had managed to lure her into his car—twenty-four long, anguished hours spent hoping her parents would find her and deliver her from this torture. Of course, she hadn't actually been able to count the hours, but she was sure of it because she could see through a narrow crack in the rock to where the sun was sinking on the horizon.

"Here, I brought you something to eat."

The girl glanced at the paper bag before turning her back on the man, trying to ignore him.

"Come on, come a little closer. Over here," he coaxed in a sugary voice. "If you're a good girl I could even untie you…"

This was beyond tempting, but the child knew what would happen to her if she let herself be persuaded. She managed to stifle a retch and to shut off her mind so she wouldn't have to think about the horrible things her abductor had forced her to do. She turned to look at the gap that led to the outside world, and let her imagination wander to thoughts of Hansel and Gretel, the characters from her favorite children's story. She was nearly at the end of the story, the bit where Gretel manages to shut the evil witch in the oven, when she noticed that the sound of scrunching paper and the glug-glug of someone drinking had stopped. She strained her ears to listen, secretly hoping the man had left, but just as she was looking round to check, the rough palm of a warm hand came down onto her freezing shoulder, making her scream in terror.

**

The cabin my parents had rented was on the shore of a lake near the Nature's Bounty Wildlife Reserve. It was the fourth year in a row we had moved into this dream location for the summer. We felt so at home here that there was even talk of us buying it. I thought this was a great idea because I'd gotten attached to the cabin's raw wooden planks and its sun-faded green metal roof. The triangle-shaped gable might have looked a bit too tall for itself if it hadn't been broken up by a wide gallery that ran around the sides of the house. This was my place of choice when I wanted to sneak off to read or daydream.

I had set myself up on the south side of the house, my fifteen-year-old self laying out on a sun-lounger, far from the distractions of everyday life. The canopy of leaves was just patchy enough to let through the right amount of light for me to read without completely dazzling me. But for now, I'd abandoned the latest must-read vampire book, and I was letting my imagination stray through the mists of love and beyond…to the delicious thrill of the dangers represented by a relationship with an undead bloodsucker. I had almost willed myself into a real-life adrenaline rush when I heard hurried footsteps reverberating on the worn wooden balcony.

"Maddie! Maddie!"

Sigh. Not easy making the most of the summer vacation when you're blighted with a nine-year-old kid sister.

"Oh, come with me, Maddie, please! If you don't, Mom'll never let me go."

"Leave me alone, Jess. Can't you see I'm reading?"

"You can finish your book after. It won't fly away."

Jessica was not only blessed with incontrovertible logic, she was also very determined. Sooner or later, she would win, so I might as well give in. Even so, I decided to wage one last battle and gain some more time.

"OK. Give me another fifteen minutes, just so I can finish my chapter."

"No! If we don't go right away, the bus for the treasure hunt will leave without us."

There was no arguing with her, so I heaved another sigh. She could see I was still in no hurry to resurface from the world of my book, so she played her winning card: "Emily's coming too…with her brother Zachary."

The wonderful music of that name made me snap my book shut. Zachary. Well, that changed everything. OK, so the thought of spending several hours in the middle of the woods looking for clues wasn't very tempting, but having this particular young man there was guaranteed to give this particular hell a candy-coating of paradise.

Emily's brother was the epitome of inaccessible. He was handsome, mysterious, and off limits. I often ended up sitting on a flat rock some way away from the clearing behind his cabin where he played his guitar with his friends, but there was absolutely no question of my joining them. Even though we were nearly neighbors, my mother had strictly forbidden it. True, some evenings they passed the beer around and the smell of some not-entirely-legal grass mingled with the lovely smell of campfire wafting over to where I was hiding. Next year maybe…I'd be sixteen then. With a bit of luck, my mother might feel like cutting me some slack. But for now, I had to admit that this treasure hunt would be a great opportunity for me. Snapping out of my daydream, I made up my mind to move, and suddenly found I was all impatience.

Jessica was so sure she had won, she was already on the phone to Emily by the time I reached the kitchen. My mother was fussing around her anxiously, and lost no time trotting out her usual mantra of warnings:

"Now, you girls better be careful. Look after each other. It's so easy to get lost in the woods. Make sure you have plenty of water. And don't forget your insect repel—"

"Mom!"

"All right, OK. But don't stray too far from the paths, and watch out for bears."

Now she really was going too far. I couldn't help replying with a casual "The last time anyone saw a bear around here was 1929."

I opened the cupboard, took out some bread, and grabbed the butter dish to make some sandwiches.

"What are you doing?" Jessica asked irritably.

"It's going to be a long day. We'll have to eat at some point."

"I have everything we need here," she said proudly, pointing to her backpack.

Jessica really had thought of everything. With a flash of rebellion, I took my time putting the bread and the butter dish away.

"Hurry, Maddie! It's nearly ten o'clock. The bus will be here any minute."

She rushed outside like a fire was licking at her heels, giving me only a couple of seconds to grab my jacket. My mother turned to face me, an anxious smile stretching the corners of her mouth.

"Promise me you'll look after your sister, Madison. You know what she's like…"

"Don't worry about it, Mom. I'll bring back all the pieces."

I gave her a kiss on the cheek, took a deep breath, and walked out the door, my thoughts already focused on this day full of promise.

The air seemed a little cool for the time of year. It was late summer now, but the sun was right where it should be. I shrugged my jacket right up around my shoulders and joined Jessica, who was hopping up and down impatiently by the roadside. The bus came around the corner of our road and coasted the last few yards toward us before coming to a halt with a grinding of brakes.

The door was barely open before Jessica bounded up the steps and disappeared inside. I climbed in behind her and said hi to the driver before heading off down the aisle. My heart did a couple of somersaults inside my chest when I realized the only empty space in the whole vehicle was right next to Emily's brother. I hesitated for a moment, and I could feel I was blushing. That was just the first of many blushes in what was to be a long day, a day that would completely change my life. But right then I had absolutely no idea about that. If I'd known…

2
The Treasure Hunt

The journey to the pretty little church on the edge of the woods seemed to go on for about a year. I spent that whole twelve months trying to control myself, doing everything I could to avoid staring at Zachary or accidentally touching any part of him as we sat side by side. Meanwhile, I wanted to keep half an ear on what Jessica was saying from the seat in front of me. She was bombarding us with information about this treasure hunt that had been set up by the local mayor. Lulled by the constant flow of my sister's increasingly detailed chatter, I let my guard down for a moment and turned to look at Zachary. Big mistake! Two huge green eyes edged with dark lashes were peering right at me, intrigued. Like a deer caught in the headlights of a car, I couldn't move. I looked right into his eyes…which is when I noticed the fine slivers of gold in the emerald of his irises.

It wasn't the first time I'd seen Zachary, but it was the first time I'd gotten that close to him. Completely captivated, I let my eyes travel slowly down his fine straight nose toward his mouth and his beautiful full lips, which were just asking to be kissed. All sorts of thoughts sidled into my mind, stoking flames in the pit of my stomach, and—oh dear—the flames reached all the way up to my cheeks.

"Did you get caught too?" he asked hoarsely, trying to break the almost unbearable tension.

"Caught?" I asked stupidly in a dreamy voice.

"Yeah, I mean with the treasure hunt."

"Oh, right…that."

Snapping out of my trance, I realized I was staring at his lips with completely inappropriate concentration, and I blushed all the harder. It was the first time a boy had had this sort of effect on me. Maybe it was because he was seventeen…

The bus chose that exact moment to go over a bump, lifting me out of my seat and practically dropping me in Zachary's lap. I totally lost my balance and flailed my hands in the air, trying to find something to grab a hold of. My fingers found the velvety softness of a blue and red sweater while a firm, warm hand closed around my waist to stop me from falling. With my nose buried in the soft knit, I inhaled a delicious lungful of a clean smell with a hint of lime. That little citrus twist made my head spin, and I realized I was breathless, as if I'd just run a half a mile.

I risked a glance at Zachary's emerald eyes again. His expression had changed, shifting from intrigued to amused.

With my heart galloping, I extricated myself from his arm and slithered over to the far side of the beige vinyl seat. Even though I was looking away, I could still feel his mocking gaze.

Determined to ignore him, I riffled through the pockets of my jacket, looking for my iPod. As soon as I found it, I popped the earphones in and turned the volume up to maximum. The opening notes of my favorite song flooded my mind and rippled through me, settling the hectic hammering of my heart. By the end of the second song, I had calmed down, and I thought I could cope with facing Zachary again. He was busy tapping away at the keypad of his cell phone, totally ignoring me, which meant I could study him at my leisure. His black hair, which was about shoulder length, made a striking contrast with my own light brown, almost blond hair. An unruly curl lolled against his cheek, partly masking his face and his strongly defined eyebrows. With an irritable flick, he tucked the curl behind his ear, revealing a small gold earring, which immediately attracted my attention. It really suited him, making him look kind of rebellious, or maybe bohemian…yes, that was the word for someone who played the guitar beautifully.

When he finished his text, he put his cell away in the back pocket of his jeans, bringing an end to my discrete investigation session. I wasn't ready to try and meet his eye again, so I turned to look out the window and tried to concentrate on the scenery scrolling past: an endless succession of boring houses with itty-bitty yards. The torture was coming to an end because we finally reached the far end of town. The bus slowed slightly and turned down the track toward the parking lot for the church. The place was already teeming with so many people, it was difficult for the driver to reach our allocated parking space.

Before the vehicle even came to a standstill, Jessica was skipping down the aisle, eager to head off into the forest and look for clues. A few moments later, the doors finally opened and let us out. When I stepped out, I waited for Zachary to join me before taking a deep breath and joining the fray, a compact crowd milling around the tables where volunteers were handling registrations. Jessica and Emily had already run over, so I decided to stay to one side and watch all the competitors while trying to ignore the delicious shivering sensation I got from standing close to Zachary.

People had gathered into small groups to discuss tactics for the treasure hunt. I recognized a few neighbors and saw that there were quite a lot of people my age, but also some adults who had gotten caught up in the excitement. It was going to be a hard-fought competition.

After what felt like an eternity, Jessica and Emily raced back over and slapped red-and-white stickers onto us, with our names and team number on them. I tilted my head down to see what number we'd been given. Twenty-one. I remembered the card game black jack, and hoped this magic number would bring us a bit of luck.

We had to wait a few minutes until one of the organizers told us we could go to the starting line along with the twenty other four-player teams. Keeping one half-hearted ear on the instructions, I started to look at the place that would be our habitat for the day: the forest. It was late morning, and it seemed quiet in there, as if the trees were holding their breath, bracing themselves for an invasion by this seething mass of human beings.

A young woman wearing a volunteer badge walked along the line, handing an envelope to each group leader. What the heck is this? I thought. And then I realized I hadn't listened to any of the explanations we'd just been given. I turned to Zachary, hoping he'd listened a little more attentively. He greeted my unspoken question with a mocking expression and a mischievous smile.

After a few moments of suspense, he consented to explain. "This envelope contains our instructions for getting to the start of the treasure hunt," he said solemnly. "Each team has a different starting point, but the finish line is the same for—"

A nasal voice blasting from a megaphone interrupted his dazzling revelations.

"On my signal, go! Off you go!"

The air was filled with the scuffling sound of twenty-two envelopes being ripped open, and the next minute, an army of clue-hunters launched into the woods to find their starting points. The whole ghastly race was underway. I heaved a deep sigh, knotted my jacket around my waist, and headed off after my teammates.

3
A Promising Start

I'm guessing Zachary had also promised to look after his sister because he outright refused to let her out of his sight. The two girls were so enthusiastic I had to break into a trot to keep up, and I was short of breath by the time I joined them beside an oak tree with the number twenty-one painted on it in large white numerals. There was a gray box sitting at the foot of the tree, waiting to be found, impatient to give up its secrets.

Jessica and Emily both reached out their hands to grab this precious box. Each refusing to give in, they started squabbling noisily until Zachary put an end to the hostilities. Boy, was this going to be a long day…

I sighed again and sat down on a fallen tree trunk, gladly surrendering management of these operations to Zachary. He battled with the lid of the box for a moment and then took out a folded piece of paper on which the first enigmatic clue was written.

"When the sun gets up, I'm lying down," he read.

Jessica and Emily looked at each other, puzzled. What could that possibly mean?

"I know!" Emily cried suddenly. "It's something in the shape of the sun that's lying down!"

She spun around, looking at the ground, trying to find something that looked like the sun. Meanwhile, Jessica, who was usually so logical, seemed to be way out of her depth. She didn't easily admit defeat, and her little face was screwed up in total consternation.

Zachary had a better idea. "What if it's something that comes out at night and sleeps all day. It could be a sculpture of an animal or something like that."

The two girls busied themselves searching for anything that might look even vaguely like an animal while Zachary stood lost in though. I made the most of this opportunity to have another good look at him. He was tall, a good head taller than me. Through the fabric of his jeans, I could see the muscles of his long legs, which were perfectly balanced by his broad shoulders and beautifully proportioned hands. He had a very distinctive way of walking. It was like there was some mystery behind his every footstep.

My gaze lingered on what he was wearing: bleached jeans and a blue and red sweater that was a bit warm for the time of year, but I'd touched it earlier and I knew how soft and comfortable it was. I had to resist the temptation to run over and huddle into that welcoming warmth. Next, I let my eyes wander back up to that mouth and those full lips that were currently curled into an eager smile. Surprised, I glanced up at his eyes and was instantly hypnotized by them. He held me prisoner for quite a while; then his velvety voice broke the spell.

"You're not helping much, Maddie…"

I stared at him idiotically. He had such a hold over me, it was terrifying. I shook my head in an attempt to break free and gather my thoughts.

"The sun rises in the east, doesn't it?" I managed. "So we need to look for something lying down in the east. Like a tree stump maybe?"

One-nil to me. His amused expression had just changed mode and gone up a notch to the impressed level. I stood up and took my time brushing some imaginary grains of sand from my jeans. Then I headed in the direction the sun would rise and stopped at the foot of an imposing old tree stump so battered by the weather that a deep hole had been carved out at its base, creating the sort of place animals could nestle. Surely some friendly kind of animal, I thought as I hunkered down to have a look… unless it was something else. Suddenly worried, I peered cautiously into the opening, but I couldn't see anything moving. Gathering all my courage, I edged closer and started feeling through the moss and wood shavings in search of clues, fully aware that Zachary was walking over slowly. Just as I caught a whiff of his citrusy smell, my hand closed around a metallic box.

Trying to steady the uncontrollable fluttering that started up the moment he came near me, I scuttled away to have a good look at the box. It was exactly like the one we'd found at the foot of tree twenty-one. I opened it and took out a folded piece of paper.

"Go fifty paces north and look for a red arrow," I read out.

"Jessica, Emily, this way!" Zachary called.

They hurried over to us.

"You found it?" Jessica almost screamed, hoisting up the straps of her backpack.

"Shush," Zachary said authoritatively. "You mustn't let the other contestants hear. That's no way to win."

Jessica looked down, mortified. Then, noticing the smile hovering on Zachary's lips, she realized he was making fun of her.

"It doesn't make any difference," she objected. "We all have different routes."

He laughed and ruffled her hair.

"Maddie found the clue," he told them. "We have to go fifty paces, starting from that tree stump and heading north. When we've done that, we should find a red arrow."

"It all depends on knowing exactly which way is north," I said.

"No problem," Jessica replied.

She swung her backpack off and unzipped the first compartment.

"Ta-dah!" she trumpeted, brandishing a small compass.

She really had thought of everything.

"Do you know how to use it?" Zachary asked.

"Of course! I learned it in summer camp. It's really easy. Look!"

She headed over to the tree stump, stood still, and consulted the instrument. With the needle pointing toward magnetic north, she started taking large strides and counting her paces.

"Fifty!" she announced. "The red arrow should be somewhere here."

We all joined her and started looking. Nothing. Not even a suggestion of a red arrow, not anywhere. After a few minutes, I gave up.

"Maybe you counted wrong," I suggested.

"Or your strides were too long, or too short," Zachary added. "Lend me your compass. I'll try."

Jessica didn't protest, and meekly watched Zachary pace out the route again.

"Fifty!" he announced in turn. "I'm pretty much in the same place as you. I just don't get it."

Jessica came over to him without a word and studied the ground at Zachary's feet. She searched for a few minutes and then crouched down to scrutinize a particular spot.

"It's not red, but that does look like an arrow, doesn't it?"

I knelt down next to her and saw a broken branch, bent into a ninety-degree angle. It was pointing toward the east.

"This must be our next clue," Zachary said, bending forward to scrutinize the branch. "It's from a red cedar tree."

"How do you know?" Jessica asked suspiciously.

"Well, I've been to summer camp too, you know."

Accepting this explanation, Jessica picked up the branch and swept aside the leaves and pine needles to clear the ground. It looked as if the earth had recently been disturbed. Using a piece of bark, she started digging, and it wasn't long before she came across one of those sought-after boxes. Clutching her treasure, she leapt to her feet and proudly showed it off.

"Found it!"

"Hurry up and open it!" Emily begged.

Jessica lifted the metal lid with almost frenetic enthusiasm, and took out one of the now familiar pieces of paper. The hunt was getting exciting, and I was beginning to get caught up in it, which gave me something other than Zachary to think about.

"I murmur while the bird sings," Jessica read out.

"I think people talk about streams murmuring," Zachary said thoughtfully.

"So we need to find some kind of water. But which way should we look?" asked Emily.

"Maybe toward the east," I offered. "That's where the red arrow was pointing."

"Good idea. Let's start by finding the water; then we'll try and come up with an explanation for the singing bird."

Jessica took her compass back from Zachary and started heading east, closely followed by Emily, who was now carrying the backpack. Pretty confident that the girls would succeed in finding a stream, Zachary and I hung back slightly. I was just in front of him, and I made myself concentrate on the woods up ahead to banish the burning sensation of having his eyes on the back of my head, my hair, my back, and maybe my…

I desperately wanted to turn around and look at him, but I managed to hold back. Then, totally unexpectedly, he drew level with me, reached out a hand, and touched my cheek. I closed my eyes to savor that gentle touch, and walked even more slowly.

"What are you thinking about?" he asked, his eyes boring into me.

"Um, nothing much," I lied, flushing slightly. "I was just listening to the birds singing."

"OK," he accepted this. "So, which is the prettiest song, then?"

He'd called my bluff, and I flushed even redder.

"Well, um…I don't know. Actually, I don't know anything about birds."

We walked on in silence for a while, listening attentively until we noticed a melodious whistling echoing through the forest.

"That one!" I breathed. "That one's real pretty."

"It is," Zachary agreed. "It's one of my favorites."

"What sort of bird is it?" I asked, listening to another burst of the harmonious song.

Zachary stopped at the foot of a maple tree and looked up into its foliage before replying, "It's a white-throated sparrow, and I think she's calling her mate."

"How do you know?" I asked, completely incredulous.

"What? Can't you hear it?" he said, looking at me in astonishment.

He turned to look up into the leaves again, and started singing, "Where are you, Frederick, Frederick, Frederick?"

I watched him skeptically, but then the sparrow sang her song once more.

"OK, all right," I conceded, more or less convinced.

Zachary replied with a mocking smile before noticing how far behind the girls we were and setting off again. I followed him, walking more quickly until I could see Emily and Jessica up ahead. Relieved, I glanced at my watch and worked out we'd been walking for a good twenty minutes. That was when I heard it: a deep, threatening growl.

Looking up sharply, I saw Jessica standing totally petrified. Twenty paces in front of her was a bear staring right at her, its lips curled back to reveal its teeth.

4
An Unlucky Encounter

I crept over to the two girls and whispered, "Don't move."

Zachary got a grip on himself and joined me as quietly as possible. The great black-haired beast was clearly angry; it was swaying from side to side, giving a muted growl every now and then. I hoped with all my heart it wasn't a female who had cubs to protect, in which case we wouldn't have any chance of surviving.

I grasped my sister and her friend by the shoulder and pulled them back so they were standing behind me. Then, I started stepping backward slowly, talking softly to the animal to try to reassure it. The bear stopped swaying and growling, but took a step forward, its lips still curled back and its nose in the air, analyzing our scent.

Jessica gave a little scream and leapt backward. I raised my hand and tried to calm her.

"There's no danger, Jess," I murmured. "He's just inquisitive. Keep walking backward slowly. If we give him some space, he should go away."

"How do you know?" Zachary asked very quietly.

"I read a lot…" I answered after a slight pause.

Not taking our eyes off the bear, we backed away, but the animal didn't look like it wanted to leave. All of a sudden, it reared up onto its hind feet, sniffing the air with palpitating nostrils.

"What's he doing?" Zachary asked with obvious panic in his voice. "It's like there's something he's interested in."

I thought for a moment and remembered my sister's backpack.

"Jessica, what did you pack in your bag?"

It took a few seconds for her to get a hold of herself before she could think back through what she had done and give us a list of what was in there.

"A can of mosquito spray, a flashlight, a map, a compass, a bottle of water, some cereal bars and some sandwiches."

"What sort of sandwiches?" I pounced on her with the next question.

"Peanut butter and honey," she admitted sheepishly.

"Well, there's the guilty party!"

Still backing away and keeping my eyes on the bear, I grabbed the backpack and started opening it so I could take the sandwiches out. I know you should never feed wild animals but I reckoned this was a pretty desperate situation and we could make an exception this once. I would just have to explain it all clearly to Jessica afterward.

I struggled for a while with my sister's ridiculously fastidious wrapping, and eventually succeeded in freeing the incriminating slices of bread oozing with honey. The bear panicked me by dropping onto all fours and loping toward me. With a little cry, I threw down the sandwiches and, losing my head, I dropped the whole backpack and fled to join the rest of the group.

I ran for some time, my mind completely blank. Low branches whipped at my face and thorny bushes scratched my thighs through my ripped jeans. All around me the forest seemed to reverberate with screams of terror. When I finally stopped running, I realized I was alone in the middle of nowhere. I leaned forward and rested my hands on my knees to catch my breath. Then I wiped away a smear of red seeping from a scratch across my cheek.

When my breathing was more or less back to normal, I listened to check that the bear hadn't followed me. Reassured by the silence broken only by the irritating sound of insects hovering around the smell of my blood, I started calling the others.

"Jessica! Emily! Zachary!"

The only answer I got was birdsong. I called again several times in vain. Tired, spent, and despairing, I slumped down onto a flat moss-covered stone and grasped the full horror of my situation. I was completely lost. I had no water, no food, and no compass, and I'd lost my teammates. I suddenly thought of my sister whom I'd promised to protect, and a sledgehammer of guilt knocked the remaining morale out of me. I sat and let the tears flow.

I'd been nursing my self-pity for a good ten minutes when I heard calling in the distance. I wiped my cheeks with the back of my hand and leapt to my feet, straining my ears to hear. Brushing aside my exhaustion and the scratches, I plied my way through the jungle of pine trees and other plants that were doing their best to get in my way.

"I'm here!" I yelled.

However loudly I cried, it felt like their calls were getting farther and farther away. Driven on by an energy born of despair, I forced my way through the undergrowth, ignoring the scrapes that each new branch etched out on my battered body.

When I came to a turn in the path, the cries sounded closer, fuelling my determination to find my friends. I gathered my strength and ran toward them until I caught a glimpse of red and blue fabric through the trees. At last! I raced over those last few yards like a thing possessed, and threw myself against Zachary's sweater, unashamedly soaking it with tears of relief. His arms closed around me immediately, protecting me. It felt so good that I completely broke down.

After a few minutes that felt both too long and too short, I looked up and got lost somewhere in those gold-flecked eyes. And there I read a combination of surprise and amusement. Suddenly aware of what I'd just done, I started struggling to free myself. He opened his arms wide to release me. I catapulted out of his hug like he'd burned me, and I turned to look at Jessica and Emily, who were sitting side by side on a rock. They were watching me, not really understanding, their eyes full of questions.

My face turned a very dark shade of red, and I had to stifle an urge to run away all over again.

"I'm sorry," I muttered.

Zachary was staring at me in silence, while my sister and her friend carried on watching me, still intrigued. Feeling acutely embarrassed, I tried to save face by taking charge of operations.

"Right, first of all, we need to work out where we are. Jessica, your compass would be very useful right now," I said, reaching out my hand.

"It sure would. If you hadn't so generously given my backpack to the bear, it would be very useful," she replied with plenty of sarcasm in her voice.

That was enough to finish me off. How could I have been so stupid, losing that precious bag with everything we needed to survive? I let myself drop down to the ground and curled up into a ball. A few minutes later, Zachary came over quietly and held out a hand to me.

"At least the bear won't get lost," he whispered.

The mental picture of the bear twiddling the compass in every direction made me smile. I took his hand gratefully and got to my feet. I brushed off my clothes, trying to restore some order to this whole mess, and looked up at Zachary. Right then, he was staring at the horizon, and there was so much determination in his expression that I was convinced we would all get out OK. At least, that's what I hoped.

5
Lost in the Woods

When you get lost in the woods, the first thing you should do, in my opinion, is find something as close as possible to a path, and follow it. So I turned in a large circle, peering into the forest. Nothing but trees as far as the eye could see. Feeling helpless, I glanced over to Zachary and saw that he'd had a better idea: he was holding his cell phone in one hand and walking around the edge of the clearing, trying to get a signal.

"Got it!" he cried suddenly, his face lighting up.

My heart loaded with tension, I watched as he punched out the emergency number.

"Hello!" he almost yelled into the phone when he heard the operator's voice. "We're lost in the woods and…hello! Can you hear me?"

A shudder of disappointment ran down my spine when I realized the call had failed.

"Try again," I insisted, going over toward the edge of the trees where he was busy pressing redial.

"Hello? Hello?

"It's no good," he muttered in exasperation after several more attempts. "There's not enough signal."

He tried a few more times before heaving a long sigh and resigning himself to putting his cell away in the back pocket of his jeans.

"I'll try later," he promised, avoiding my eye. "But in the meantime, we need to find another solution."

I watched him surreptitiously, my heart fluttering. He was walking toward Emily, looking thoughtful, his expression as unreadable as a slab of marble. But I had the feeling there were a few cracks and flaws disturbing the cool calm of that marble surface. I shivered nervously. If Zachary was cracking up, I didn't hold out much hope for us. Everything would depend on my ability to make the right decisions, and I wasn't sure I was up to getting us out of this fix. I set about biting one of my nails, feeling the full weight of the responsibility bearing down on my shoulders. I seriously needed to pull myself together and find a solution.

I feverishly turned around in a circle again, looking at the forest, but that curtain of green obstinately refused to open for me and reveal a path. Next, I closed my eyes and took a deep breath, forcing myself to calm down. After several slow, deep inhalations, I opened my eyes and looked at the edge of the woods in front of me again. After looking more slowly and methodically, I spotted a gap between two maples that looked like it might be a pathway. I was about to open my mouth to tell the others when Zachary spoke before I had the chance.

"I think the best thing to do would be to find a stream. We're not far from the river here. Any streams we find must feed into it."

He was right. If we could make it to the river, we were saved.

"Good idea," I said, my fears somewhat relieved. "Which way do you think we should head?"

"It's just after midday. The sun should be in the south," he said with newfound confidence. He looked up and pointed toward the sun, adding, "I think we should head that way."

"Bad idea!" came a voice behind us.

Zachary and I turned around simultaneously.

"And why's that, Miss Know-it-all?" I asked, turning to look at my sister furiously. Her unexpected intervention was threatening to sap what little confidence we'd managed to restore.

She returned my stare coolly for a while before explaining, "Because the sun isn't necessarily due south at midday."

"What do you mean?" asked Zachary, suddenly not so sure of himself.

"It depends which time zone we're in," she said in a teacher-like voice. "And it also depends on exactly where we are. The sun will be in the south somewhere in our time zone, but not necessarily here."

Her implacable logic put a stop to any more questions.

"And anyway," she added, getting to her feet, "the sun will move. So if we follow it, we could end up going around in circles."

"Well, what do you suggest then?" I asked. "You do have an idea, don't you?"

She met my eye for a few seconds more, and then her chin started to wobble and silent tears trickled down her cheeks. She looked away.

"I don't know," she mumbled quietly. "We never got lost at summer camp."

My heart thumped hard in my chest and I had an urge to put my arms around her, but I quashed this instinctive gesture. I'd just seen Zachary's confidence waver. I felt the worst thing I could do was to soften and succumb to my emotions.

I thought for a moment, weighing the various options open to us. The first was to stay here and hope to be saved, but with no food or water, it was likely to be a long wait, possibly even a fatal one. By the time someone realized we were missing, organized search parties, and actually found us, we could be there many hours, or even days. Of course there was the call Zachary had almost succeeded in making, but I very much doubted the operator had managed to establish our whereabouts. So we had to move, if only to find the things we needed to help us survive.

"I think I have an idea," I announced eventually, breaking the heavy silence that had settled over us. "I've spotted a path nearby. With a bit of luck, it could be a route used by animals to get to a source of water. I think we should follow it, but keep an eye on the sun. And obviously we'll try not to go round in circles," I added, glancing at my sister.

"OK," Zachary agreed after a moment's deliberation. "Anything's better than just staying here and waiting."

I set off, hoping it looked like I was walking with conviction. Zachary made the girls go ahead of him, and we headed toward what I hoped was a track. When I came to the gap I had spotted some minutes earlier, I parted the branches and was relieved to find a path. The woods were dense but there was a narrow pathway picking its way through the trees.

Jessica wriggled through first and started following the path tentatively, with Emily so close behind her that they looked almost surgically joined. Still holding the branches back with one hand, I waved Zachary on; then I brought up the rear.

The sun filtered through the leaves, but it was hard to keep heading south. We had to follow the twists and turns of the path, snaking through rocks and trees. Unlike humans, animals tend to take the easiest route, so their tracks aren't always straight. At least the slight downward slope and the pleasant temperature meant we wouldn't dehydrate too quickly. The mosquitoes, on the other hand, were torment. They buzzed around us constantly, adding to the dizzy feeling we had from being tired, thirsty, and hungry. After three hours like this, we were walking like zombies, unable to think about anything except putting one foot in front of the other.

To be honest, this state of mind suited me just fine. It meant I didn't have to think about Zachary or the embarrassing way I'd reacted when I found them all again. Just remembering how I'd thrown myself into his arms was enough to make the blood rush to my cheeks. I had the distinct impression I'd been betrayed: this body I'd been living in for fifteen years was completely out of my control every time I came within ten feet of Zachary. It was frustrating but intoxicating at the same time— and scary too. Like I was a prisoner on a fairground ride climbing up to the last summit on a rollercoaster before launching into thin air. That image was enough to set my heart beating to a hectic rhythm again. I tried to calm it down by thinking about something else.

Zachary tripped, annihilating my efforts not to think about him. He only just managed to keep his balance, but the harm was done. My eyes had been dis-tracted from the ground and were now focused on him. I studied his wide shoulders and imagined them with no clothes on. I had no trouble picturing how his muscles would be moving as he walked. My imagination was now out of my control, and it was growing bolder by the minute. My gaze drifted slowly down the length of his back and stopped on his buttocks, which were round and firm. As if alerted by a sixth sense, he turned around at that exact moment. Of course I looked away, but Zachary's sardonic smile made it clear I wasn't quick enough. The guilty pleasure must have been written all over my face. Feeling very flustered, I missed my footing, tripped on a tree root, and fell flat on the ground.

Ever the valiant knight, Zachary was quick to reach out a hand, the corners of his mouth curling up another notch. Furious with myself, I ignored his offer of help and got to my feet. A sharp pain shot through my ankle when I put my foot to the ground. I gave a little cry and fell down again. Zachary's smile melted away.

"Are you OK?" he asked, concern creeping into his expression.

Stupid question. Of course I wasn't OK! I wanted to answer him in an angry, disdainful voice, but it too was betraying me now, and all I managed was a feeble, "I've twisted my ankle…I think."

"Let's have a look," he said, taking my leg with some authority.

I pushed his hand away and tried to stand up again. He sat me back down gently but firmly, and started unlacing my sneaker. I couldn't disguise a grimace of pain when he eased my sneaker and my sock off. I noticed his sly smile, though, and looked down to see my azure-blue toenails. It had seemed such a good idea during my pedicure session with my friends; now it was just embarrassing. Painting your toenails isn't a crime in itself, but Zachary's mocking expression had this uncanny way of making me feel awkward. I snatched my foot away and put my sock back on to hide the incriminating nail polish.

"It doesn't look too bad," he said, standing up. "But I can carry you if you like…"

The very thought of it was enough to heal me instantly and completely. I would walk until my foot fell off the end of my leg if need be, but there was no way Zachary would be taking me in his arms. I'd die of embarrassment. Or happiness…

My ankle was starting to swell, but I ignored it and put my sneaker back on. Still refusing Zachary's outstretched hand, I got back to my feet painfully. I'd been worried I wouldn't be able to put my foot to the ground, but the pain was actually bearable. I limped off down the track, and we joined Jessica and Emily, who had slumped to the ground to rest a little way ahead.

6
The Stream

Zachary ran the last few yards when he realized his sister was crying silently. He leaned over her and took her in his arms, trying to communicate some of his energy to her. Then he looked up and caught my eye. We looked right into each other's eyes, and I read in his a reflection of my own fear, but something else too. Something like regret.

My brain was dulled by tiredness but it tried its best to decipher what his expression meant. What did he regret? What might have been? It was true that, with our lives in danger, the chances of making more of this attraction between us were looking pretty slim. But was there really an attraction? Did Zachary feel the same way? Wasn't it just my unbridled imagination galloping off on the flights of fancy? I so longed for romance that I dreamed up all sorts of things.

I banished these ridiculous thoughts from my mind and turned my attention to my own sister. Jessica was sitting a little way away, and but she looked to be coping with this ordeal bravely. Her love of sport meant she had developed more endurance than I had, but the fact that she was so young meant she was more likely to crack eventually. I put my injured foot to the ground with a grimace of pain and went over to her.

"You OK? You holding up?" I asked.

She shrugged but didn't say anything: a sign that she wasn't OK at all. With a sigh, I dropped down beside her and put my arms around her. I gathered together all my resolve and put as much confidence as I could muster into my voice.

"I'm sure there's already someone looking for us," I said. "The emergency services should find us soon."

She gave another shrug of her shoulders and turned away from me slightly. I held her all the closer to boost her morale, and felt a tear drop onto my hand.

"Jess, it's going to be OK. I promise you they'll find us."

"This is all my fault," she managed quietly. "If I hadn't insisted we take part in this dumb treasure hunt, none of this would have happened."

So that was it. This was the first time, to my knowledge, my sister had experienced any sense of guilt.

"You're kidding, right?" I replied, trying to play things down. "Before we ran into the bear, it was kind of fun, wasn't it? And now it's turned into something even more exciting."

She turned her face sharply to look at me, her eyes incredulous.

"Exciting?"

Then she noticed my sly smile and realized I was joking.

"Come on," I said, getting back to my feet. "If we're going to get out of this mess, we need to keep moving."

"OK."

She looked more like herself again as she got to her feet beside me, and the two of us went to join our partners in misfortune.

Emily was in a bad way: Zachary was holding her in his arms, and she was sobbing almost hysterically. He looked up as we came over, and I could see how worried and powerless he felt. Jessica crouched next to her friend and started whispering words of encouragement. She carried on with such persistence and conviction that she got the better of Emily's tears. It wasn't long before she was helping Emily to her feet and we could continue on our way.

The path was a little wider now, which nurtured my hope that it was used regularly and would lead us to water. Jessica held Emily's hand, and they walked along side by side, a long way ahead of Zachary, who had drop-ped back because he was concentrating so hard on the screen of his cell phone.

I'd been lost in my thoughts for several minutes, when something brushed against my hand, sending an electric shock through the tips of my fingers. The buzzing sensation insinuated itself into my blood vessels and wormed its way up my arm. A shudder of pleasure rippled through my whole body when the electric current reached the pit of my stomach.

"Are you cold?" asked Zachary, who was walking next to me now.

His deep, velvety voice set off another little shudder.

"I'm fine," I said, and it wasn't a lie.

But he didn't believe me. He took my hand firmly and held it prisoner in the warmth of his. His hand felt soft yet strong. I caught my breath, in too much turmoil to speak.

"How old are you?" he asked after several minutes' silence.

It was tempting to add a couple of years to my age. More than tempting. But I resisted the temptation.

"I'm fifteen," I said, shamefaced.

The verdict wouldn't be long coming. I expected him to release my hand and move away any minute. He digested the information for several seconds before bringing an end to the suspense.

"You seem older. I'd have thought you were at least sixteen…" he said, tightening his hold on my hand.

My heart skipped with joy. I was so happy I had to look away for fear he would read the delight on my face. That was when Emily collapsed for the second time.

Zachary dropped my hand and ran to his sister. The poor girl looked completely exhausted.

"What's the matter with her?" Jessica asked, turning to look at me anxiously.

"She's too tired to keep walking," Zachary explained. "I'll have to carry her."

Our romantic interlude had just come to an end. I couldn't help giving a long sigh of disappointment. But I immediately felt very guilty when I looked at Emily. She seemed to be in such bad shape that I silenced my regrets and focused on more urgent concerns.

"Can you keep on trying?" Zachary asked, handing me his cell phone.

"Of course," I said, taking it from him, glad to be kept busy.

I glanced at the screen and was disappointed to see that there was still no signal at all. But it was the icon right next to the signal that made my stomach contract. The battery was almost flat. I looked up to tell Zachary, but decided not to say anything when I saw him picking up his sister and struggling to get to his feet again. I prayed we would find water soon, because the way he swayed as he walked made it clear he wouldn't be able to carry Emily for long.

Another problem was looming on the horizon. The sun had started to go down, making the temperature drop several degrees. I huddled my jacket closer around my shoulders and held out my hand to Jessica. She rewarded me with a grateful smile and eagerly clung to my arm. Her eyes, which now had dark rings around them, darted about anxiously the whole time.

The ground had originally been more or less flat, but it was now heading slightly uphill, and the path was dotted with occasional rocks that we had to clamber around. The forest seemed to be waking, giving off random rustlings and whisperings. If we didn't get out of the woods soon, we would have to come to terms with the idea of finding shelter for the night.

A sudden growling sound startled me. Zachary and Jessica must have heard it too because they stopped in their tracks to listen. Oh my God, what could it be? A wolf? A shiver of terror brought goose bumps out in my skin. Could there be wolves in a wildlife reserve? Well, why not? There sure were bears, weren't there? I couldn't help remembering our unlucky encounter, and that cranked my fear up another notch. I put my arms around Jessica's shoulders and hugged her to me.

We waited for a while in the fading daylight, but we didn't hear the growling again. On the other hand, our silence meant we could now hear another sound we hadn't noticed before: a constant murmuring. Like water…

Zachary, Jessica, and I looked at each other in disbelief. Then my sister darted on ahead with newfound enthusiasm. A few moments later, we heard her whoops of joy, and we ran as best we could over the uneven surface, guided by her voice.

7
Meanwhile, in the Cave

When she felt the man's hot breath on her neck, the little girl gave a sharp scream and started shaking like a leaf quivering in the breeze.

"So you do have a voice," he whispered quietly. "I didn't know I'd have to make you scream to hear it…"

He sniggered as he stroked the child's back. With her skin puckered in disgust, she brought her knees up to her chest and backed away till she was pressed up against her bound hands. She wanted to get as far from the man as possible, but his warm breath caught up with her straightaway.

"Come on, don't be difficult," he wheedled. "If you're a good girl, I won't hurt you."

Curling up even tighter, the girl blocked him out of her mind and went off onto another flight of fancy in the world she had created for herself, with Hansel and

Gretel. This time, she was quickly brought back to reality by the sound of voices. Thinking she must be dreaming, she strained her ears toward the opening in the rocks. It sounded like children shouting. The man had heard them too, and he'd stopped what he was doing to listen to them.

"Shit," he muttered.

He clamped his hand over the girl's mouth and snarled, "If you make a noise, I'll kill you. Get it?"

She nodded her assent, two big tears rolling down her cheeks. The man withdrew his hand cautiously but soon replaced it with a piece of cloth that he stuffed between her lips. He knotted this makeshift gag at the back of her head and left the cave.

**

Jessica was already leaning over the stream when we reached her. Her hair was trailing in the water, and she was gulping great mouthfuls, coughing from time to time.

"Stop, Jess! You'll make yourself ill," I cried, running over to her.

"She's right, Jessica. The water may not be drinkable," Zachary agreed, putting Emily down.

Her cheeks pink with guilt as if she'd been found with her hand in the candy jar, Jessica stepped back, wiping her mouth on her sleeve. It wasn't a very wide stream, but I had to admit the water looked irresistibly clear. I knelt down beside my sister and cupped some water in my hands. It was clean and it had no smell. I dipped my tongue in it: there was no taste either.

"It seems OK," I announced, looking up toward Zachary.

"It's hard to know for sure," he said. "But one thing is sure: if we don't drink soon, we're risking being in even worse shape."

"You're right," I said, bending down to the stream.

I took some water in the palm of my hand and drank a few mouthfuls. That cool liquid running down my throat made me feel like I was being reborn, and I sighed with contentment. I just couldn't stop myself taking more and quenching my terrible thirst.

Emily leaned down to slake her thirst too. With one hand on his sister's shoulder, Zachary held back her hair with the other so she could drink more easily. After a few minutes, I thought I could see some color coming back into her cheeks. Only then did Zachary plunge his whole head into the stream, reemerging immediately and flicking back his hair. He showered Emily with water, and she laughed. Drawn by her friend's cries, Jessica jumped up and ran over to share in the fun.

With a smile playing on my lips, I walked away slightly to avoid being splashed, and I sat back down by the edge of the stream. I took off my sneaker and sock to have a good look at my ankle. It wasn't as swollen as

I'd thought. I'd been careful to put my foot down straight with every step, and the effort had paid off.

With a sigh, I shuffled closer to the water and put my lower leg into the stream. The cold felt wonderful, and the pain ebbed away.

"How's your ankle?" Zachary asked, coming over to me.

"Fine," I lied to avoid getting into the subject in detail.

"Please let me have a look at it," he asked, dropping down beside me.

I looked right into his eyes, searching for any signs of sarcasm, but could only see slight concern and genuine interest. I surrendered and took my foot out of the water so that he could have a look. Zachary put his hand gently on my lower leg and ran it softly over my ankle. The touch of his palm against my bare skin set off more uncontrollable shivers, which snaked all the way to my stomach, and I had to resist a sudden urge to close my eyes and savor the feeling. My body wanted more, and for a moment I was worried Zachary would be able to hear my heart pounding. Luckily, he seemed to be totally focused on examining my ankle. At least that's what I thought—until his hand traveled slowly up to my thigh…

His eyes met mine. His pupils were slightly dilated and they held mine prisoner. Now I really didn't know which way to turn. That moment felt so fragile, as if the slightest sound, the slightest movement would burst this timeless bubble. I sat absolutely motionless and stared into his eyes, which looked down at my mouth. My lips trembled open as he drew imperceptibly nearer. Just as he was finally tilting his head toward me, I closed my eyes and—

"Where's Jessica?" Emily asked, bursting the bubble.

For one infinite second, my heart stopped beating. Zachary let go of my leg and leapt to his feet as if his life depended on it.

"I don't know," he said, trying to clear his head. "Isn't she with you?"

"No. I'm not sure, but I think she went that way," she pointed toward the north.

I dried my ankle as best I could, trying to keep calm so the blaze of red in my cheeks would die down. Then I put on my sock and sneaker before reckoning my voice would be firm enough to break the silence that had settled over us.

"I'll go look for her," I offered, tying my laces.

"OK," agreed Zachary, who seemed to have pulled himself together. "While you're doing that, I'll look for firewood."

I nodded and handed him his cell phone. His eyebrows shot up when he saw that the battery was dead, but he didn't comment on it, and put the cell in his pocket before going over to a tree with bare, gnarled branches.

I stood up and headed in the opposite direction. Jessica was inquisitive but, given the circumstances, she wouldn't have gone far. I limped on, walking upstream, scanning the undergrowth for signs of my sister while my mind tried to unscramble my confused thoughts. Had Zachary tried to kiss me? I felt my cheeks blazing again. No, maybe he'd just tried to get closer to explain something more clearly.

I took a few more steps as I mulled over this possibility. Was I sure of that? He'd stroked me with his hand, hadn't he?

Hearing someone call my name, I jumped, interrupting my ruminations.

"Maddie! Maddie!"

"Over here!"

Jessica bounded out of the trees, flushed from running. Her dirty face and unkempt hair made me feel a surge of affection for her, and that set my thoughts back on the right track.

"Look what I found!" she said proudly.

I went over to her and tucked a stray lock of hair behind her ear.

"Let's see," I said, my voice softened by an instinctive need to protect that every big sister feels.

She uncurled her fingers to reveal her treasure. In the crook of her hand a few juicy raspberries were waiting quietly to be eaten. My heart leapt for joy at the sight of them, and my stomach rumbled.

"Where did you find them?" I asked, suddenly feverish with energy.

"Just there, behind the rocks," she replied, pointing with her free hand. "There are lots more. Hey, could you take these to Emily? I'm going to pick some more."

"OK. But be careful. Don't get too far away."

In no time, she had dropped her treasure into my hand and gone.

8
Back in the Cave

The little girl froze, all her senses alert. The shouts from outside the cave had stopped so she focused her attention on the inside, but there too it was silent. The man who was holding her prisoner had been gone quite a while now and seemed in no hurry to come back. She looked down at the ground and patiently went back to the task she had assigned herself. Every time the predator had left her alone, she had rubbed the rope against a rock behind her back. She had worked methodically and now the ties were beginning to give way.

The rock had sharp edges and they had cut her. Her blood mingled with sweat and burned the tender skin on her wrists, but she barely even noticed. The discomfort was nothing compared to what the man would do to her if she didn't manage to escape. She paused for a few moments to twist her hands in every direction: yes, there was a new slackness in the rope. Fired up by this glimmer of hope, she gritted her teeth and started rubbing the rope against the rock again.

The silence was suddenly broken by a squeaking sound that made her jump. She froze again and listened, her every muscle taut with fear. The noise came again just above her head; she huddled into a ball and listened intently. Eventually, she realized it must be some sort of animal she had disturbed, probably a bat. Ignoring this invisible companion, she went back to her dogged work.

A few minutes later, all her efforts were rewarded: the last shreds of rope tore and her hands were free at last. She circled them for a while to restore the circulation before grappling with her gag, which was soon on the ground with the rope.

She stood up stiffly, resting her hand onto the wall of rock to steady the head rush that nearly made her fall over. The dizziness went on for several minutes, fading gradually, and this proved to her how terribly weak she was. She absolutely had to escape before the man came back, because she clearly wouldn't be able to stand up to his considerable physical strength.

Having more or less regained her balance, she eased along the wall of the cave toward the suggestion of light coming from the opening. She had no idea which way to go because she had been unconscious when her kidnapper brought her here. But for now she knew which direction to take because there seemed to be only one narrow gallery leading toward the glimmer of light from the mouth of the cave. She slipped into this gallery and vanished in the darkness.

She travelled along the tunnel for several yards before hearing footsteps. With a shiver of terror she waited motionless until she saw a glow of light a long way down the tunnel, confirming her fears: the footsteps were coming toward her.

Not sure what to do, she bit her lip as she tried to decide: should she go back to the chamber and pretend to be tied up so she could wait for the right moment to escape, or would it be better to keep going in the hopes of finding a recess she could hide in?

Unable to tolerate having her tormentor around her a minute longer, she rushed forward looking for a hiding place. She took a few steps to the right and noticed a crack in the wall of rock. It seemed wide enough for her to slip into. She twisted sideways and managed to get almost all of her body into the fissure. Now all she could do was wait and hope the man didn't happen to look in her direction.

The footsteps became clearer, and the darkness gradually gave way to the beam of a flashlight. The girl shrunk into herself and completely stopped breathing. But as the predator passed, she couldn't restrain a tiny whimper of terror. The man stopped dead and turned to look in her direction. Their eyes met. A scream of anguish exploded inside the child's head, and her whole body was instantly flooded with fear. A powerful dose of adrenaline accelerated her heart rate and gave her a few seconds of total lucidity. She knew what she had to do and her reflexes responded: she sprang out of the crack in the rock like a jack-in-a-box.

She just managed to escape the man's clutches but one hand trailed behind for a moment too long. The predator snatched hold of it with a cry of fury and started hauling the child toward him. She fought him off with an energy born of complete desperation. Her wrist was slick with blood and was difficult to grip so she managed to slip free of his grasp and run away along the dark tunnel. With her attacker on her heels, she raced along the gallery of rock and came out of the mountainside shrieking in terror. She carried on running for several minutes, then slammed into something hard and collapsed on the ground.

9
A Little Girl

I got back to my feet with some difficulty. A canon ball had just barreled into me, knocking me to the ground, and I'd dropped the treasure my sister had so patiently picked. I thought briefly of Emily's exhausted face, and I felt a pang of regret. But I soon drove away this thought to focus on my current situation: a little girl was sobbing convulsively at my feet.

I knelt down and drew aside her long tangled black hair. She cried all the more desolately and curled up into a ball. I rested my hand gently on her back to try to calm her, but she screamed with fear. I immediately withdrew my hand and stood up, powerless. I heard someone running and looked up to see Zachary hurrying over, drawn by the girl's screams.

"Who's that?" he asked hoarsely, trying to catch his breath.

"I don't know. She only just got here!"

"Got here" was quite an understatement, I thought, remembering the force she'd come at me with, felling me like a tree.

Emily seemed to be feeling better. She was still pale, but she'd followed her brother and was leaning over the little girl, talking to her. Her gentle voice was more effective than my would-be soothing gesture had been, because the girl gradually grew calmer. Emily helped her sit up, and put her arms around her, which only made the girl cry more. But her sobbing had changed, as if she'd switched from fear to relief. I let Emily comfort the girl awhile longer before going up to her again and moving the hair off her face. She recoiled instinctively, like an animal caught in a trap, but she let me touch her. I allowed plenty of time for her to get used to me; then I ventured my first question:

"What's your name?" I asked, reckoning this was the best way to start.

She didn't reply, but looked away and clung to Emily. Right. OK. I abandoned my attempts and stood up again; I thought I should give her more time. OK, so it was pretty strange to find a little girl in the depths of the forest, but she didn't necessarily represent any danger.

"What do you think?" I asked, turning to Zachary.

"I really don't know," he said. "It's kind of weird…"

"Weird?" I laughed out loud. Was there anything normal about this whole day?

A sharp scream coming from the stream cut my laughter dead. Jessica…

As if animated by a life of their own, my legs set off first, dragging me along with them down to the water. Zachary was right behind me and nearly knocked me over when I stopped abruptly, my eyes bulging in horror. A man was holding my sister by one arm and threatening to cut her throat with a knife.

"Don't come any closer!" he yelled. "Or I'll kill her."

My heart seemed to stop beating completely. His instruction had robbed me of any desire to move, not even a single hair on my head. My eyelids remained open and my eyes were pinned on Jessica's little face. She was white as a sheet and looked as if she might collapse at any moment. Her body was wracked with uncontrollable shuddering and her cheeks were streaked with tears of terror. The kidnapper looked about ready to break down himself. His feet shuffled constantly, crushing the raspberries my sister had just picked. Those bleeding berries were more than I could take, and my tears started to flow.

Zachary stood motionless, pale as a corpse. His mouth had opened to form an O" of astonishment, and he was staring so intently at the predator that I honestly wondered if it was possible for a person to be turned into a statue. The fact that a man like this had appeared deep into the woods was truly horrible, but there was something about Zachary's reaction that I found disturbing.

I wondered exactly what was going on with him when the man spoke to him.

"Well, well…Zachary…" he drawled sardonically.

Now my mouth opened to form an O of its own. My eyes darted backward and forward between Zachary and my sister's kidnapper. I managed to draw in a breath to demand some sort of explanation, but I exhaled slowly, unable to formulate a single word.

A stifled cry from behind my back made me turn around. Her eyes wide with horror and her face ashen, Emily had fallen to her knees with her hands clamped over her mouth. I couldn't see the little girl we'd found anywhere, but I was sure she wasn't far away.

Knowing Emily was there seemed to release Zachary from his trance. He took a step forward and tilted his chin as he confronted the predator.

"Let her go," he shouted, his voice ablaze with anger.

"Stay where you are, asshole," the man replied, tightening his hold on my sister.

"Let her go right now! If not—"

"If not what?" the man interrupted with a sneer.

He started backing away, dragging Jessica with him, while she moaned softly. I looked up at Zachary, who didn't dare do anything more. He was opening and closing his hands convulsively and shaking from head to foot.

I could see he wasn't going to be any help, so I had to do something myself. There was no way I could let this man leave with my sister without trying to do something. I took a deep breath to build up my courage, and made a great effort to control the emotion in my voice.

"Wait!" I cried, a tremolo betraying my panic.

The predator slowed down but didn't stop.

"I can offer you a trade," I suggested, relieved that he was at least listening to me. "You let her go and I'll be your prisoner."

The kidnapper sniggered contemptuously and carried on walking. This rejection made me all the more desperate. Without thinking, I took a step forward; my instincts told me that if I let Jessica go now, I was squandering my chances of seeing her alive again. I took another step, but this only unleashed the man's anger.

"Stop!" he yelled, tightening his grip on my sister. "Another step and I'll kill her. I mean it. I'm taking her with me, whether you like it or not."

The predator was clearly about to snap. His face was a deep red color and, despite the distance between us, I could see the dark rings of sweat on his faded blue shirt. I watched utterly powerless as he gradually disappeared through the trees.

"Don't come after me!" I heard him calling, his voice muted as he drew farther away. "I'll kill her, I tell you."

I let a few minutes go by, torn between a longing to follow the attacker to snatch Jessica back from him, and the fear that I'd be condemning her only chance of survival. My hearing was so acute now that I could still hear the man struggling and Jessica whimpering. When I could no longer hear anything, my fears got the upper hand and I ran into the forest.

I searched for several minutes, stopping every now and then to listen, but Jessica and her kidnapper had completely disappeared. Deep down, I knew that the longer this went on, the less likely I was to find them. After half an hour, I accepted that it was too late and I'd lost Jessica forever. My mind in turmoil and refusing to accept the facts, I carried on searching and frantically calling her name for several more minutes.

The truth finally caught up with me, and the horror of what had just happened bore down on me. The strength drained out of my legs, and I dropped to my knees, struggling to breathe. I'd promised to look after my sister and I'd failed terribly in that promise. The feeling of guilt was so strong, it nearly suffocated me. But another feeling, one I had not experienced before, gradually cut through all other emotion: pain. I loved Jessica with all my heart, and I'd just lost her forever. The pain that weighed down on my chest was so unbearable that I sprawled on the ground, sobbing helplessly.

10
A Terrible Secret

I stayed like that a long time, crying till I thought I must have no tears left. Then a fleeting memory surfaced in my mind. Jessica's kidnapper had used Zachary's name, so he must know him. And if he knew Zachary, then there was a strong chance Zachary knew him.

The incalculable pain crushing my heart gradually gave way to a glowering rage. Zachary knew who the attacker was, and he'd done nothing to stop him taking my sister away. The fury that now gripped me restored my strength and got me back on my feet. I angrily dusted off my clothes and impatiently swiped the tears from my face. Zachary had better have a good explanation…

But before I could bombard him with my anger, I needed to find him. I looked up and scanned the forest around me, hoping to orient myself. In my panic, I had flitted frantically in every direction, and I now had no idea where I was. I closed my eyes to calm myself, and stood motionless for a few moments. As far as I knew, I'd been going around in circles more or less in the same area, so I couldn't be very far from the stream. After listening for a while, I managed to make out a vague murmuring sound. I opened my eyes and set off in the direction of this faint sound.

It was dark now, but a feeble orange glow still lit the woods enough for me to get my bearings. It wasn't long before I found the stream, and I strode purposefully along it for several minutes. Despite the pain in my ankle, this forced march did me good and went some way to quieting my anger. I still felt just as much resentment toward Zachary, but at least I was prepared to listen to his explanations.

Turning a corner in the path, I was hit by the smell of wood smoke, which meant Zachary had succeeded in lighting a fire. The relief that I had found them and would soon be warming myself by a fire quickened my pace. After one more turning, I could see the flames at last.

Emily was sitting on the ground, huddled up to the little girl we'd found. The poor child was wearing only her underwear, and she looked frozen. Emily turned around when she heard me, and the relief lit up her tired face.

"Maddie!"

Her cry of joy reverberated around the woods, disturbing some sort of animal, which shifted in the undergrowth. Remembering our encounter with the bear, my blood ran cold.

"Shush!" I said, standing between the two girls and the noise.

The scrub rustled more loudly, and the animal emerged from the woods, its mane matted and its arms laden with wood intended to feed the fire. The site of Zachary calmed my fear but reignited my anger, and I could feel the resentment flashing in my eyes. Zachary's smile of relief froze on his lips. He knelt down and offloaded his heavy cargo. I couldn't wait any longer before laying into him with my first question:

"What do you—"

The look he shot me silenced me automatically. His eyes flitted anxiously over to Emily, and looked back up to mine imploringly. Then he looked away with such finality and determination that I knew it would completely pointless trying to get anything out of him right away.

I held my anger in check for now, and appropriated one end of the makeshift seat Emily was sharing with her new friend. Zachary still had it coming to him; I would just bide my time until we were away from his sister's prying ears.

Wanting to concentrate on something else, I turned to look at the girl we'd found—or rather, who'd found us. Her dark brown eyes were staring at me through the curtain of hair that she kept permanently over her face. She was quite little and couldn't have been more than seven or eight years old. She was wearing a torn, stained tank top so her arms and shoulders were bare. Her panties were in no better state, and she had only one sock. The fire was giving off a good amount of heat but hadn't completely stopped her shivering. Unless the shivering was caused not by the cold, but something else.

I stood up and took off my jacket to put it around her shoulders. I hadn't yet warmed up myself, but I thought she needed it more than I did. This didn't seem to frighten her, so I knelt in front of her and gently swept aside the hair hiding her face. She leant a little closer to Emily, but didn't shrink away from me. Her eyes were no longer filled with terror like the first time I tried to get near her, but you could feel the fear hovering just beneath the surface, ready to surge back up at any moment. Right now she didn't look like she was about to run away, so I risked trying to speak to her again.

"What's your name?"

She took a while to speak, searching through her memory with a frown, as if wondering whether she even had a name. Because of this long silence and her dark coloring, I thought maybe she didn't understand English. But she eventually answered in a pretty voice with a hint of a lilting accent:

"Isabella," she breathed quietly.

This effort of concentration seemed to have completely exhausted her. I drew in a breath to ask her another question, but she closed her eyes and huddled up to Emily, who glanced at me apologetically. She looked to be at the end of her tether too. I sighed and stood up, looking for Zachary, who seemed to have vanished.

I heard a twig snapping, and headed off in that direction. I soon found him, breaking up pieces of soft cedar wood. I wondered what on earth they could be for, and then a mental picture of Zachary and me arm in arm on an improvised bed came to me, making me look away in shame. Furious with myself, I blotted out this unsettling image and tried as best I could to ignore the glow it had ignited in the pit of my stomach.

While I pulled myself together, I started helping Zachary and tried to fire up the anger that had swept over me when the predator took my sister. But the pain and confusion I could see in Zachary's eyes when he looked up at me fuelled only a very pale copy of the rage that had possessed me. My heart felt heavy in my chest, and it was with a much gentler voice than I would have wanted that I finally asked, "Who was that man?"

Zachary carried on with his work for a while, apparently weighing up his options. Then he sighed and almost whispered the words, "He's my father."

Too stunned to manage any sort of response, I watched Zachary break the last of the branches and slink off into the trees. He'd been gone for some time before I got a hold of myself again. Zachary's father had abducted my sister. And Emily's father was the same person as Zachary's father. What I had just worked out made no sense, but, thanks to the day's dreadful events, my mind was so alive to the extraordinary that it had grasped the facts.

I felt like a fog was hanging over me, and I tried to shrug it off by picking up a few pieces of wood Zachary had missed. With the soft wood in my arms, I drifted back to where the others were.

The fire was crackling merrily now, and there was cedar wood scattered all over the ground around the fallen tree the girls were using as a seat. I walked over and added my share of the haul to the other branches making up an improvised bed. I had to admit that this makeshift resting place looked tempting.

Suddenly overwhelmingly tired, I knelt shyly next to Emily. She immediately moved closer to me to make the most of my warmth. I put an arm around her and glanced surreptitiously at Isabella, who clung to her new friend like a strip of sticky tape.

Isabella. What in the world was she doing here? Did she have something to do with Jessica's kidnapper? Or had she simply gotten lost too? I thought about her half-naked body and the fear widening her eyes, but refused to make a connection with Zachary's father. That would be way too horrible…

I shivered and huddled a little closer to Emily, unable to drive away images of rape flitting across my mind. Then my thoughts turned to Jessica. My heart skipped a beat and all the blood drained from my face. Filled with sudden panic, I stifled a cry and looked up toward Zachary.

We looked right at each other, my eyes brimming with tears, pleading with him to allay my worst fears. For a few moments, I felt he opened up to me, letting me read deep inside him, where I found answers to all my questions. Then his face seemed to shut off, and he went back to the task he'd assigned himself.

11
A Visitor in the Night

Several hours passed before I became aware of my surroundings again. On top of my fear, hunger, and exhaustion, the fact that my sister had been abducted had snuffed out the last spark of clear thinking left in my head. I had curled up and withdrawn, completely anesthetized. I hadn't really slept, but just disappeared into a painful in-between state, as if two hands had grabbed a hold of me and tried to pull me in different directions: one toward reality, the other toward dreams that allowed me to forget. It was the weight of a warm body pressed up against me that snapped me out of this state.

I held my breath and felt Zachary go still beside me.

"I just want to get warm," he whispered.

It would have been cruel to push him away, because it was really cold. So I let him lie right up against my back, and I felt the warmth of his sigh of relief on the nape of my neck. I could feel him gradually relax, and a few minutes later, his steady, regular breathing implied that he was fast asleep.

There was no way I would get to sleep now. Having Zachary this close was so unsettling that I was likely to start quivering again. Once I was sure he was fully asleep, I allowed myself to enjoy this un-hoped-for proximity. I broke out in goose bumps and gave a little shiver. That was when I realized I'd been wrong: Zachary wasn't actually sleeping. My shiver must have made him think I was cold, because he moved even closer and put his arms around me. Now I knew I wouldn't get a moment's rest all night. But exhaustion got the better of me, and, to my considerable surprise, I eventually fell asleep.

**

Fetid hot breath hovering over my neck woke me from my restless slumbers, making me almost retch in disgust. Stifling a scream, I sat up and looked around. Emily and Isabella stirred slightly but they were so exhausted, they didn't wake. They shifted into a more comfortable position and sank back into a deep sleep. Zachary was awake, though, and was up on one elbow, peering at me questioningly. I was just trying to untangle dreams from reality, when the terrible smell drifted over me again, this time teamed with a barely audible growling sound. Zachary wrinkled his nose and sat up too, but only very slowly, listening the entire time.

The fire had almost gone out, leaving our surroundings in darkness that a slender crescent moon failed to illuminate. I could feel my heart pounding, and a cold shiver ran up and down my spine. I reached blindly for Zachary's hand, and when I found it, it held mine tightly. His strong, firm grip reassured me, and I moved closer to him. I opened my mouth, a question hovering on my lips, but he put a finger to his mouth to tell me to stay quiet.

After a few moments' silence, we were startled by a rustle of leaves. Whatever this animal or thing was, it had decided to move away. Zachary let go of my hand slowly, as if not wanting to, and got up to stoke the fire. Reassuring, warming flames soon sprang up again.

"What was that thing?" I asked, staring at Zachary who'd just sat back down.

"I have no idea. A wolf maybe?"

"Well, if it was a wolf, it had terrible breath…"

"Yeah. I'm gonna try not to think about what he'd eaten."

I shuddered with disgust at the thought.

"Are you cold?" he asked quickly.

"No, I'm fine. It's just the thought of a wolf who…"

"I see."

He moved over to me and held me close, his arm tight around my shoulders. The warmth radiating from his body gradually calmed my shaking. I leaned against him and relaxed, acutely aware of the feelings he awakened in me. It was the first time a boy had had this effect on me. As well as making me clumsy, he seemed to stop me from thinking rationally, which gave my imagination plenty of space to go off at a tangent, projecting uncontrollable images inside my head: kisses and more, things I could never own up to. But another image, the memory of Jessica's terrorized little face, was still too fresh in my mind for me to give in to these fantasies. Instead, I decided the time had come to ask some questions.

"So what's the story with your father?" I asked, backing away slightly.

Zachary looked at me for a few moments, clearly surprised; then his face went blank. He too moved away a little, and leaned against the fallen tree, gazing into the fire and distractedly bending and unbending a pliable twig. The flames danced against his profile, throwing orange patterns over his cheeks. After several minutes' silence, I realized he wasn't planning to answer any questions. I opened my mouth to insist, but Zachary cut in, making me jump.

"I haven't seen him for nearly two years," he started with a hoarse crack in his voice. I wanted to ask him more questions but resisted the temptation; that might stop him talking altogether. He was clearly finding this difficult: I could see the emotion playing on his face. His jaw was clenched as he fought to restrain what looked like anger. After several minutes of inner struggle, he mastered his emotions and went on with his explanation.

"That night two years ago, the night he left, I'd woken up because I heard Emily crying. I thought she must have had a nightmare or something like that. My mom was working late, so I got up to comfort my sister. But when I reached her bedroom, my dad was already there. He was with her, in her bed…"

Zachary stopped, unable to continue. I could tell he was shaking with anger and a sense of his own powerlessness.

"He was, you know, assaulting her," he blurted, turning toward me and raising his voice to add, "Do you understand what I'm saying?"

The horror of what he'd just said still didn't stifle the surge of tenderness I felt for him, seeing so much pain in his eyes. I reached out my hand to take his, but he brushed mine aside and moved farther back against the tree trunk. When he had calmed down a little, he went on more quietly.

"I yelled at him, and I beat him. So he packed his bags and he left."

His voice cracked again. He was balling his fists, fighting desperately to control his emotions. I gently put a finger to his face to wipe away the single tear trickling over his cheek. He turned toward me, leaning his cheek into my cupped hand. This took me completely by surprise, and I looked right into his eyes. That was when I knew I was totally lost.

I took his face in my hands and put my lips to his. His mouth was warm and soft but hesitant at first. Then the emotion he'd been holding back for so long was unleashed in his kiss. His lips tightened, expressing his fury, before growing impulsive and demanding, trying to satisfy the urgent need for tenderness that I sensed in him. He pressed his body right up against mine, wanting to mold to my every contour.

It was only one kiss, but it awakened longings in me that I'd never experienced before. My hands moved over his body, responding to his caresses. It was as if my body had a life of its own and was acting independently of my mind…which was yelling at me to stop. A tell-tale hardness in Zachary's pants was all it took for me to lose myself completely. I pressed myself against him and started to rock my hips and moan.

That was when Emily screamed.

12
The Cave

Emily's screams had the effect of a cold shower on me. I gathered my wits in a fraction of a second and pushed Zachary away. In a flash, he was by Emily's side, taking her in his arms. Seeing him consoling his sister reignited my deep-seeded, heart-breaking feelings of guilt for failing to protect mine. I'd been so obsessed with being in Zachary's arms that I'd blanked out the whole episode of her abduction. A sledgehammer of remorse smacked into me, and I bit one of my nails right down to the quick.

In an attempt to shrug off the confusion in my mind, I gazed deep into the fire. On the far side of the fire, Isabella had curled up on herself, shivering and pulling the collar of my jacket close around her neck. Her dark eyes had grown so large with fear that they seemed to take up most of her exhausted little face. My heart overflowed with compassion at the sight of her, and my big-sister instincts—that were so mortified for failing Jessica—begged me to redeem myself as best I could by taking care of this lost child. I went over to her slowly, with the softest, kindest expression in my eyes. The little girl's frightened eyes locked onto mine, and her obvious distress blew away my last shreds of hesitation. I leaned over her and took her in my arms.

Her tiny frozen body tensed against me at first; then I felt her succumbing to my warmth. Her sudden trust produced a surge of tenderness in me, going some way to relieving my feelings of failure and powerlessness. I held her a little tighter, hoping I had enough courage in me to confront the hunger, the cold—my own contradictory emotions and the last shadowy hours of the night. A deep sense of calm flooded through me, and it took my mind several seconds to register what had caused this unexpected serenity…although my body knew perfectly well. Without even meaning to, I'd just found an effective defense against the dangerous power of attraction Zachary exerted over me.

As if equipped with a sixth sense, Zachary looked up at that exact moment. His green, gold-flecked gaze peered into my eyes and studied me, trying to understand the newfound self-assurance he could sense in me. My sudden coolness was completely at odds with the feverish way I'd responded to his kisses only moments before. I looked away and turned my face up to the sky.

A diffuse light had started to whiten the horizon. There was absolutely no point lying down and trying to sleep now, and it was by general consensus that we decided to set off again. We put out the fire and started walking upstream. That was the direction in which Zachary's father had disappeared with Jessica, and there was no way we were leaving this forest before we'd found my sister. We walked along the stream for a good twenty minutes before Isabella started to make little moaning noises beside me. Remembering she didn't have any shoes, I thought the rough path must be hurting her feet, and I leaned down to take her in my arms. A dull pain throbbed through my ankle, and I had to put her down again, but she just curled up into a ball on the ground.

"I don't think she can go any farther," I said, turning toward Zachary, who was close behind us. "And I'll never be able to carry her."

"OK," he said, bending down toward Isabella.

The child gave a scream and clung to my legs, whimpering. Emily rushed over to reassure her, whispering soothing words in her ear, but Isabella refused to let go. After several minutes of resistance, she finally agreed to let Zachary carry her, and we set off again.

Only a dozen or so paces farther on, Isabella buried her face in Zachary's shoulder and sobbed. A couple more strides, and she was really screaming and struggling. Zachary shot me an apologetic look before putting her down.

"What is it?" I asked her, crouching beside her. "Where's it hurting?"

She didn't answer, but moaned pitifully, staring at the opposite bank of the stream. That was when I noticed an opening in the rock. It was the deep, wide mouth of a cave, and was relatively close to the place where Jessica had been abducted. Could there be some connection between this cave and the predator? I spun round to face Zachary, my eyes full of hope.

"Well, it's worth checking," he agreed, guessing what I was thinking. "You stay here with the girls; I'll go have a look."

The thought of being separated from him sent a shiver of anxiety through me. I was pretty sure I would have what it took to fight off Jessica's kidnapper, but God alone knew exactly what lay in store for Zachary in that cave. Just the thought of it made my heart race frantically. Either way, there was no question of my staying with the two girls without him.

"I'm not OK with this," I said, my voice quavering. "We shouldn't split up."

"It's better if I go alone," he insisted, misunderstanding what was worrying me. "If I need to get out in a hurry…"

Zachary didn't have to finish his sentence. I could see what he was thinking: if we needed to run, Emily and Isabella could put us all in danger.

"OK, sure. But be careful," I conceded, accepting the facts.

My concern put a flicker of surprise in his eyes, like it was inconceivable that I might worry about him. The sly smile I so dreaded teased the corners of his mouth and brought a flush to my cheeks.

"You too," he called as he set off across the stream.

He was at the mouth of the cave within seconds and soon disappeared into the dark tunnel. The long wait had started.

Emily and Isabella sat down to rest on the edge of the stream, which was strewn with pebbles. I dropped down beside them and started building a little heap of the almost perfectly round stones. I was bored of this pointless exercise within only a few minutes and tried to find something else to keep me busy.

My stomach was grumbling, reminding me of a nagging hunger that had been making me feel giddy for some time. I suddenly remembered Jessica revealing her handful of raspberries with a triumphant flourish, but the image was so painful that I tried to blot it out. Scenes of rape scrolled through my mind, adding to my torment, breaking my skin out in horrified goose bumps. I shrugged convulsively, trying to drive away these disturbing images, praying desperately that Mr. Morgan, Zachary's father, wouldn't hurt my sister.

I couldn't bear the inactivity any longer and thought I could explore our surroundings, but when I put my hand to the ground to get up, the idea of leaving the two girls alone stopped me in my tracks. I very much doubted Mr. Morgan would try to get anywhere near us, but what about the creature that had visited us in the night? The smell of it was still far too fresh in my memory. There was still a chance the thing was lurking nearby, and I started glancing around anxiously. I was patrolling the edge of the woods by eye when I thought I saw something move. I stared at the spot for a while, but the bushes stayed perfectly still. Maybe it was just the wind in the leaves…

I stood up and started walking up and down the riverbank. I had the distinct impression we were being watched, and I even thought I could smell the repulsive animal. Growing more edgy by the minute, I paced up and down more quickly, chewing another nail right down. I thought I saw a movement behind a bush and stopped dead, probing the undergrowth with my eyes. Something brushed against my shoulder making me scream with fright. I spun round, all guns blazing, and my eyes brimming with tears of terror met Zachary's astonished expression. He opened his arms wide, and I threw myself into them without any further encouragement.

13
A Ray of Hope

Zachary didn't push me away, and I made no effort to escape his hug. With my nose buried in his sweater, I cried out all the fear and relief that had been brimming inside me. Having sobbed and gulped for several minutes, I eventually lifted my head from his chest with some regret. I was too embarrassed to meet his eyes, with their ironic expression, so I kept my eyes lowered as I turned away. He took my chin in his hand and turned my face toward his. Now I could see his eyes were full of tenderness and concern, and that gave me a warm feeling inside.

"What is it?" he said gently.

I drew away slightly, trying to pull myself together and make sense of what it was that had upset me so much. But as I looked around, all I could see was a perfect summer morning: birdsong was mingling with the murmur of the stream, and a gentle breeze tickled over my skin, warmed by the rising sun. Wherever I looked, I saw nature in all its resplendent beauty.

"Nothing," I said eventually. "My imagination getting away with me, I think."

Zachary's lips curved into the sardonic smile I'd learned to dread. My cheeks started to go crimson, and I flashed him a resentful look before spinning around and running back over to Emily and Isabella, who were sitting so quietly I'd almost forgotten about them. They were busy rummaging through a big brown canvas bag and didn't appear to have noticed that I'd left them alone.

Zachary came over to join us, his amusement gradually fading as he faced up, once again, to how serious our situation was.

"I found a chamber in the cave," he told us. "There's no one there right now, but someone's obviously been living there, and I think I know who it is."

He shoved the canvas bag with his foot, as if too disgusted to touch it.

"I brought some stuff," he said, gazing away from us toward the far side of the stream.

Emily gave a little whoop: she'd just found a cereal bar, and she started yanking off the wrapper. She closed her eyes and bit into one corner with a blissful sigh. Meanwhile, Isabella had recoiled from the brown fabric as if it had scalded her. Her attitude confirmed my suspicions as to the identity of the bag's owner.

I knelt down to have a look at what was in it. I took out three cans of soda that literally made me salivate, two ham sandwiches that still seemed pretty fresh, and a few more soft cereal bars like the one Emily was eating. Well, that reassured me on one count: whatever else happened, at least the problem of what to eat was temporarily out of the way.

Continuing with my inventory, I felt some sort of fabric and pulled it out of the bag. It was a pair of jeans for someone a lot smaller than me. I opened the folded blue denim and realized they were child-sized, sort of Isabella-sized. They had to be hers.

Blotting out the horrible images that kept trying to sneak into my head, I fumbled around in the bag again and found a t-shirt, a fleece, and a pair of sneakers. Zachary must have come to the same conclusion as me, because I could read the disgust on his face.

I had no idea how the child would react when she saw her clothes again, but thought it would be best for her to put them on. I was very relieved to find that she accepted this, and she gazed passively into the woods while I dressed her. When it came to her sneakers, I remembered she was wearing only one sock. I dived back into the bag and turned the thing inside out, but it was no good. The missing sock wasn't there. She must have lost it when she ran away from her kidnapper.

Hoping she wouldn't get blisters from wearing her sneaker on a bare foot, I finished dressing her and offered her half of one of the precious sandwiches.

"Here," I heard him say as I stood up, "this is for your ankle."

He was holding out a roll of elastic bandaging.

"Thank you," I said, taking the roll from him.

I sat down on the ground, took off my shoe, and bandaged up my ankle to support it. Feeling much more comfortable, I put my sock and sneaker back on while Zachary divided the remaining sandwiches into equal portions.

We sat eating for a few minutes, listening to the noises in the woods. There was something soothing about the whispering wind rustling through the leaves in the treetops. Despite our terrible situation, I managed to relax. Zachary opened a can of orange soda and handed it to me.

"What should we do?" he asked, resting those gold-flecked eyes on me.

"I don't know," I said, trying to meet his eyes without blushing. "We could wait here. Do you think he'll come back?"

Zachary looked away and thought for a while before replying, "To be honest, I'd be very surprised."

He gazed blankly at the spruces along the edge of the forest, thinking.

"Now that we know who he is," he went on, "he won't take the risk of showing up here again. I think we'll have to try and find him. With any luck, we could even come across some help. There must be people looking for us now."

There was no arguing with that: now that we'd spent a night in the woods, a rescue party would definitely have set out to find us. My mind flitted briefly to my family's comfortable log cabin, and I caught my breath at the thought of my parents. I could picture my mother in tears and my father pacing helplessly in the dark. I didn't dare think what would happen to me if I came home without Jessica. I prayed desperately that the kidnapper had let her go and that she was back home, safe and sound. I put so much longing into the plea that I ended up believing it was possible. This hypothesis gave me strength, and I tucked into my last mouthful with new determination. One thing was sure: there was no way we could spend another night in the forest because, in my case, the animal lurking in the undergrowth wasn't the only danger that lay in store.

I stood up, sparking a look of surprise in Zachary's eyes. He watched me for a moment, and then asked again, "So, what are we doing?"

"We're getting out of here!" I replied firmly.

He watched in amazement as I gathered up our things and got Emily and Isabella to their feet.

"Is there anything else useful in the cave?" I asked, snapping him out of his torpor.

He shook his head and stood up slowly, helping me pick up the packaging and empty cans. We put them away in the canvas bag and decided to leave it there, despite a little stab of guilt for leaving it in this beautiful place. The fact that we might have to carry the girls was a good enough reason not to burden ourselves with useless trash.

Zachary led the way, closely followed by Emily and Isabella, who were holding hands. I brought up the rear, keeping my eyes and ears open. The air temperature was cooler again, but a dazzling sun was warming us with its life-giving beams. Gentle birdsong and the sounds of the stream traveled along with us, allowing us to forget our perilous situation for a while. I was surprised to find myself taking a deep breath and thanking the heavens that I was alive. We'd had a terrible night, but, still clinging to my visions of Jessica safely back at the log cabin, I had a feeling that all would be well by the end of the day. We just had to get out of the woods. The thought of that brought a smile to my face, but it was soon wiped away by the buzzing sound of a cloud of bluebottles.

Zachary was standing a few paces ahead, and he'd raised his hands to stop the girls going any farther. He was staring at something a little way in front of him on the track. I walked on a few more yards and made out something lying on the ground.

"Stay here," he said.

I crouched down and put my arms around the girls, trying to turn them away from what I thought must be a dead animal. A deer perhaps? Or maybe a bear?

Out of the corner of my eye, I watched Zachary as he walked slowly up to the body, pinching his nose. He stopped beside it and looked at it for several minutes; then he fell to his knees, shaking his head in disbelief and sobbing.

I immediately thought of Jessica and a desperate scream burst from my lungs. No!

With my mind numbed in fear, I abandoned the two girls and stumbled like a zombie to where Zachary was. My heart was thudding against my ribs, and my eyes were wide with horror as the body came properly into view. Frozen rigid for all eternity, what was left of Zachary's father lay on the ground, staring at me in grizzly silence.

14
The Corpse

With my mind completely blank, I dropped to the ground beside Zachary and took him in my arms. Even though the macabre sight of this dead body made me shudder in horror, I couldn't take my eyes off it. Mr. Morgan's corpse was still clothed, but part of it had been eaten by something. And judging by the size of the bite marks, that something was big—very big, even.

His face was intact, but his eyes were fixed open in an expression of pure terror, as if he'd been eaten alive. I'd heard various gory stories about bears, but I couldn't quite picture any ordinary animal doing a thing like this. It was horrific. Really horrific. Still, that was small potatoes compared to the idea that was trying to wriggle its way through the defensive barriers I'd carefully constructed around my subconscious—barriers that were threatening to collapse at any minute to reveal a reality I just couldn't contemplate. A reality that would destroy me forever. What had happened to Jessica?

Zachary pulled himself together first and automatically turned toward his sister. Probably out of some sort of survival instinct, the two little girls hadn't moved an inch. They'd stayed right where I'd left them. Zachary tried to peel my arms off him, but my muscles had frozen into rigid blocks of granite. He tried to talk to me, but I just didn't respond. My mind had drifted off to another planet and disconnected from this world. In the end, he shook me hard enough to free his right hand, and he slapped me.

I gasped in surprise and stared at him in bewilderment as my tears finally began to fall. I sat there stunned for several seconds before gradually emerging from my trance. We looked deep into each other's eyes for a moment, both devastated, and then stood up slowly and walked away from the corpse. That was when the first aggressive drops of rain splattered onto us. We were startled by a flash of lightning immediately followed by a clap of thunder, and hurried over to the two girls we'd abandoned behind us on the track.

Perfectly in tune with our own emotions, the sky opened up to allow the elements free reign. The storm came from nowhere. We didn't stand a chance: in a few minutes, we were totally drenched. We looked like we'd thrown ourselves into the stream. Zachary and I each took one of the girls by the hand and ran to look for somewhere to shelter. There wasn't a single cave or even crack in the rocks. We raced upstream, searching frantically, but there didn't seem to be anywhere, not even a dense tree to offer us a little protection. After a few minutes, hailstones started pelting down. The little balls of ice nipped our skin like thousands of needles. Emily and Isabella screamed, cranking up our panic another notch.

Continuing our frantic, haphazard search for shelter, we eventually found a conifer with branches that reached almost to the ground. I hesitated for a while because the dry space under the branches looked far too small. A sudden smell of sulfur followed by a spectacular thunderclap made us all scream out loud. The dazzling streak of lightning had struck very close by, and Zachary unceremoniously bundled me under the branches. I struggled awkwardly into our improvised shelter with Isabella, trying to leave enough room for Emily and Zachary. By wriggling and contorting ourselves, the four of us managed to squeeze into the makeshift refuge, and we waited in silence for the storm to pass.

A few minutes later, the elements started gradually abating, leaving us shell-shocked, soaked, and frozen. It was still raining, and the pine needles over our hideaway were not dense enough to carry on protecting us. Zachary extricated himself from under the tree and hauled me behind him. Ignoring the pain throbbing through my ankle, I took Isabella in my arms. Zachary picked up Emily, and she nestled her head in the crook of her brother's neck as we set off again, trying not to think about what the weather had just thrown at us. I had no idea what it would do next—it wasn't like I'd heard a forecast—but one thing was sure: if the sky didn't stop pouring all this water over us, we wouldn't survive another night. We absolutely had to get out of the forest. And we had to get out quick.

Shivering in every limb, I did my best to follow Zachary. The rain came down in relentless curtains, slowing us down with every step. We walked as quickly as we could, but the girls weighed heavily on us, ebbing away our strength. Adrenaline had kept me going for a while, but now that there was no immediate danger, I didn't think I could carry on like this for long.

Another few minutes passed, and the woods seemed to look a little brighter. I tried to peer through the fog of rain, but everything around me was still hazy. I slowed down to focus properly because I thought I saw a dark shape shifting through the trees. The thing moved and then stopped, as if it had seen me. It stayed still for a moment and then started coming toward me. My survival instinct flashed the image of Mr. Morgan's body into my brain. I saw him as clearly as if he'd been there at my feet. My terrified heart accelerated frantically, and a new dose of adrenaline pumped through my bloodstream. Overwhelmed by panic, I shot forward as if the very devil were on my tail. My terror brought out my instinctive self-preservation, blotting out all other considerations, and I dropped Isabella in my desperate efforts to escape the predator.

I ran as fast as I could through the trees, which became more widely spaced as I went. The rain was still obscuring my vision, but I could see clearly enough to avoid crashing into a tree trunk. Every time I looked behind me, I saw the creature's shadowy shape drawing closer. I ran all the faster, but my poor exhausted body was starting to give in. Deep down, I knew that any minute now I would collapse, and that would be the end of me.

Refusing to give up, I tried to keep going as I threw one last glance over my shoulder. My eyes wide with terror, I glimpsed the thing that was gaining on me. I ran on a few more yards before my foot caught in a tree root and I fell flat on the ground. I didn't have the strength to get back up, so I closed my eyes and waited to be eaten.

15
The Beast

When a paw landed on my shoulder, I shrieked in terror. The thing turned me over brusquely, but my next scream faltered in the back of my throat. A face with two blue eyes was peering down at me, full of concern.

The man was clearly a police officer, but his uniform was hidden by a big black raincoat.

"Are you OK?" he asked.

I couldn't manage an answer, and I saw him reach for a mouthpiece on his shoulder.

"It's OK," he said into the contraption. "I found her. I repeat, I found her."

"Ten-four."

He held out a hand to help me up, but I was so dazed I couldn't operate any of my muscles. My heart was still beating manically, having apparently not yet absorbed the fact that I'd been saved. Assuming that I was in no fit state to stand up, the police officer bent down to pick me up in his arms. Feeling his hand under my knees was enough to bring me back to my senses.

"It's cool, I can walk!" I squeaked, trying valiantly to scramble to my feet.

"Are you sure you're all right? I can carry you, you know."

"Yeah, yeah, I'm really fine," I insisted, shivering from top to toe.

Eyeing me skeptically, the officer held me by the elbow to help me to my feet. Then he led me gently back the way I'd just fled. The rain had stopped, but I was so cold my whole body was shaking. My brain had now grasped the fact that I was out of danger and had sent out orders for me to stop secreting adrenaline. Deprived of the last vestiges of this precious hormone, I felt as if I had lead weights on my shoulders. I was so tired, I had stars dancing before my eyes.

Emergency vehicles were flashing red and blue lights over the surrounding trees, and I could see people gathered around a patrol car. Suddenly painfully aware of my injured ankle, I limped along, leaning rather more than I wanted to on the officer's sturdy arm. The last few yards felt like several miles, but I managed to negotiate them, exhausted as a marathon runner tottering over the finish line.

A volunteer put a blanket over my shoulders and rested a hand over my head to make me lean forward as I stepped into the car. The officer who found me sat down beside me, and the car set off for the hospital. The shaking gradually subsided and my brain started functioning normally again. I couldn't quite believe we'd been saved. Well, not all of us…

After a few minutes, I found the courage to speak up.

"Did you find my sister?" I asked in a quavering voice so quiet I wasn't even sure the officer had heard me.

"Yes," he said with a reassuring smile. "You're all safe and sound. But you really need to see a doctor."

He patted my shoulder and turned to look at the road ahead. With my last fears dispelled, I huddled more comfortably into the blanket and dropped into a restless sleep.

**

A sudden jolt woke me from a horrible nightmare. The journey from the woods into town had never felt so quick. The car had only just stopped outside the hospital's main entrance when my door swung open and a helpful hand reached in to ease me out. I was escorted to a stretcher and helped onto it to lie down. Then I was wheeled to the emergency department, where nurses busied around me, checking my temperature and blood pressure, and examining me for fractures and injuries.

Through the sort of fog hanging over my mind, I could feel my damp clothes being removed and replaced with a hospital robe. Someone lay me back down on the stretcher, promising that a doctor would be with me soon, and the long wait started. My dazed senses needed rest, but I fought against falling asleep. The only thing I wanted right now was to be totally sure Jessica was safe. I knew she was somewhere in the hospital, safe and sound, but a tiny part of me needed to see her with my own eyes.

I stopped the first nurse who came by.

"Excuse me, do you know if I can see my sister?"

"No, I'm afraid the doctor has to examine you first," she told me.

"Please! I really need to talk to her," I persisted.

"Just a wait a little longer. It won't be long."

"Could you at least tell me where she is?"

The nurse heaved a deep sigh before making up her mind to comply with my wishes by pointing to a closed door.

"She's in that room right there."

She scuttled off busily, turned a corner, and disappeared from view. The moment she was out of sight, I threw off the covers and put my feet to the ground. The door in question wasn't very far from my stretcher. I waited a moment, swaying on the spot and checking the corridor was empty, before shakily walking over to the door. I pushed it open gently, slipped into the room, and closed the door quietly behind me.

I found myself at the foot of a bed where I could see a figure covered in a blanket, softly lit in the half light of the room. My sister must have succumbed to exhaustion because she seemed to be sound asleep. I stepped toward her silently to have a good look at her face. Her dark curls were spread over the pillow, framing her head with a black halo—except there was something wrong. Jessica was blond. I came closer and realized the nurse had it all wrong. The girl sleeping in front of me was not my sister. She was Isabella.

I backed away and left the room, making sure the door didn't slam for fear of waking her. I saw a nurse's station over to my left, and walked up to it, trying my best to keep the gap at the back of my gown closed over my naked body.

"Excuse me," I said, interrupting an animated conversation between two nurses. "I'm looking for my sister Jessica."

"Oh my! What are you doing here, miss? You need to go lie down."

"I don't want to lie down!" I almost screamed. "I have to see my sister."

"What's going on here?"

I spun round to see a man coming over, and was hugely relieved when I recognized the police officer who found me in the woods.

"It's my sister, I can't find her anywhere," I said with escalating panic in my voice. "You told me you found her."

"Calm down," he said, holding me by the arms. "Come on, let's go over here."

A quick glance around was enough to make me obey him: people had stopped mid-conversation to stare at me. One man lying on a stretcher had even raised himself onto an elbow to get a good look at me. I felt the color rise to my cheeks as I followed the officer over to a row of empty chairs. He made me sit down and put a reassuring hand on my shoulder.

"We found all four of you: Zachary and Emily Morgan, and you and your sister," he said slowly and patiently. "Jessica's sleeping in her own little room right next door to you."

That was when I realized the unthinkable had happened. The police officers who saved us had made a mistake. They'd found Isabella and taken her for my sister.

Meanwhile, Jessica was still out there in the depths of the forest.

16
Homecoming

.Back on my stretcher, I tried to sleep so that I didn't have to think. My tired brain totally refused to make any sense of my thoughts. I let myself drift off into a sort of haze where nothing could get to me. I'd just been subjected to two hours of questioning, and it had completely exhausted me. I'd tried my best to answer the machine-gun-fire questions from various police officers, but only one key fact emerged: Jessica was still out there, lost in the forest.

When my parents arrived, things hadn't gotten any better. My mom's hysteria sent me right into a bottomless pit of remorse. I was so mortified that I felt I didn't even deserve to live. And I'd walled myself up in a deep, deep silence that nothing and no one would ever be able to break down.

After several hours' wait, the doctor finally came to examine me. Apart from a sprained ankle and mild dehydration, he didn't seem that worried about me physically. He seemed a little more preoccupied with my muteness and my lethargy, but he felt it would be way better for me to go home than to spend a night under observation at the hospital. So, toward the end of the afternoon, I found myself clinging feebly to my father's arm as I walked through the door of our house.

The green-roofed cabin that I had come to love suddenly felt oppressive. I felt that every single one of the trees surrounding it was leaning in toward me to get a good look at the contemptible creature I'd become. The carefree teen had given way to a complete stranger: a dark, gloomy person who'd lost all will to live.

Oblivious to the birdsong around me and the warm breeze on my skin, I limped up the few steps onto the huge terrace that ran the length of the building. I didn't even look at those familiar faded wooden boards as I stepped inside and hurried up the stairs to the mezzanine I shared with my sister. A quick glance through her open bedroom door sent me even deeper into depression. I went into my own bedroom, collapsed on my bed, and went to sleep with my head buried in my pillow.

✳✳

It was four a.m. when I emerged from my deep sleep. Somewhere in the depths of the house, I could hear my mom's stifled sobbing and my dad's murmur of comforting words. Unable to listen to this evidence of my parents' unfathomable pain a moment longer, I put on some warm clothes and snuck downstairs. Grabbing my shoes on the way past, I padded across the kitchen, opened the door, and vanished into the darkness.

It was an even colder night than the night before. The rain had stopped, but there was still a biting wind. A mental picture of Jessica shivering and making desperate efforts to warm herself tried to cut through the hermetically sealed barrier protecting my mind, but I managed to drive it away. For now, my only chance of survival was to blot out any memories and thoughts that reminded me of my sister.

I went down the steps to the little path and followed it off into the shadows. The world around me had fallen quiet, perfectly matching my blank state of mind. The moon looked as empty as my head, and was shedding no real light, but over toward the east, I could make out a pink glow heralding the first signs of dawn, which would soon be waking the forest.

My eyes gradually adjusted to the darkness, and I set off along a track that I knew by heart because I had taken it so many times. It led to the clearing where Zachary and his friends liked to gather around a campfire. But tonight there was no smell of smoke and no sound of guitar playing lightening the gloomy atmosphere. Everything felt dead. As dead as my heart. Even thinking about Zachary's laugh couldn't raise the tiniest spark in me. I felt as if an endless, boundless ice field had descended on my entire existence—an ice field that nothing and no one would ever be able to shift.

A branch snapped to my right, startling me. I stopped and held my breath, suddenly regretting having ventured so far. Then a lighter flame briefly lit up a face that I recognized immediately. Zachary was leaning against a tree trunk, staring at me in the darkness. After a few seconds of silence, he came over and joined me on the path.

"I didn't know you smoked," I said, blurting out the first thing that came into my head.

"You wouldn't. I only just started," he replied, taking a drag on his cigarette.

We walked on a little way before either of us made up our mind to break the silence again.

"I'm so sorry about your father…"

"No," he interrupted me with an abrupt flick of his hand. "I'm not sorry."

"But…"

"It's true. And I don't want to talk about it."

There was another silence, even weightier this time. We let it fill the space between us until Zachary succeeded, with just one word, in shattering the barrier I'd so carefully constructed around my heart.

"I'm so sorry about your sister…"

Those words, pronounced with such gentleness, had the same effect on me as a tsunami. A wave of pain was unleashed inside me, sweeping aside my efforts to lock my anguish away in a sealed corner of my mind. This torment combined with a raging anger and grabbed a hold of me as I turned to Zachary and yelled at him furiously, "Yeah, and I don't want to talk about it either!"

I could feel the tears streaming down my cheeks, and turned and fled back toward the cabin. There was no way I was letting anyone see how fragile I was. Especially not Zachary. But I only ran a few yards before he caught up with me. He reached for my shoulders, automatically threw aside his cigarette, and took me in his arms.

I couldn't hold back the freight train of sorrow hurtling through my heart any longer, and I gave in to long, heaving sobs. It felt like I was crying for a whole eternity; eventually, though, my sobs came more slowly. My heart was blown apart, but the fog that had settled inside my head was gradually dissipating. It suddenly dawned on me that if Jessica wasn't found, I would never survive. So I made a big decision there and then: whatever it cost me, I was going back into the forest.

Gently extricating myself from Zachary's arms, I wiped my cheeks and looked up into his eyes. They were full of concern mingled with something else that, at the time, I couldn't quite decipher. Every ounce of me yearned to succumb to the warmth of his arms, but my determination was stronger even than that. So long as Jessica was in danger, I wouldn't be at peace.

I tactfully pushed Zachary away.

"What's going on?" he asked, aware of the change in me.

"Nothing," I said elusively.

"Well, that's just not true. Something's changed."

"I've just had an idea."

"Which is?"

I wasn't sure if I should tell him. Of course, it was sensible for at least one person to know where I was planning to go, and there was no way I could tell my parents. But, probably with good reason, I was worried about how Zachary would react. After meeting his insistent stare for several seconds, I resigned myself to explaining my plan.

"I've decided I have to go back into the forest to bring Jessica home," I said simply.

"No chance!" he roared. "There's already a search team out there."

"Yeah, but I have this feeling I'm the only person who can find her. If I don't try, I'll never be able to live with myself."

"That's a no!" he yelled, holding me so tight it hurt.

"Why?" I yelled back at him. "It's none of your business."

"Well, that's what you think!"

He snatched at my hair and rammed his lips against mine. For a moment I struggled under the pressure of his kiss, but my body eventually gave in without my consent. I clung to Zachary and totally capitulated. His mouth grew softer and his tongue edged between my lips, giving me a taste of his spicy tobacco. An unfamiliar feverishness spread through my veins, igniting a delicious quivering feeling through my whole body.

At that precise moment, I could feel Zachary losing control of himself. He held me so close, I was suffocating, and his tongue probed my mouth with hungry urgency. I moaned with pleasure and pressed myself closer to him, wanting to melt into him completely. After several minutes, Zachary relaxed his grip and broke away from the kiss breathlessly.

"At least let me come with you," he whispered in my ear.

As I tried to make sense of what he'd just said, I realized I'd completely forgotten about Jessica. I stiffened with fury and fought my way free from his arms.

"Oh no! It's way too dangerous," I replied with a forcefulness that surprised even me.

"Oh really? And what about you? Isn't it dangerous for you?"

"It's not the same! Jessica's my sister."

"That's not the point. If I can't go with you, you're staying here," he said firmly.

"And exactly how do you think you're going to stop me?" I asked triumphantly, but he took me in his arms and administered a second kiss even more lingering than the first. After a while, he let go of me, and I nearly crumpled to the ground. I felt like a puppet that had suddenly lost its strings. Zachary caught me just in time before I fell.

"If you go without me, I'll find you. I'll tie you up and I'll kiss you till you beg me to stop," he threatened.

"OK," I said hoarsely, not sure whether I was agreeing to his following me or hoping he would subject me to the punishment.

"Good. Wait here. I'm coming back."

And he disappeared among the curved branches of the tall pine trees.

17
Back in the Forest

Ten minutes later, Zachary returned, nonchalantly swinging a rifle in his left hand. He was carrying a backpack that looked quite heavy, and was chewing furiously on a piece of gum.

"I decided to stop smoking," he explained in reply to my enquiring expression.

That made me smile, and I was very happy to hold the hand he held out to me. With Zachary by my side, everything felt possible.

"Where do we start?" I asked after we'd walked a little way along the path that was feebly lit by the dawn light.

"I think we should go back to the cave. With any luck, we'll find some clues that could help us."

"You don't even know where it is," I said, mildly amused.

"How about you? Do you know, then?" he retorted.

I snatched my hand from him and pretended to turn away, but he caught me by the shoulder and drew me back next to him.

"Come on; come here," he said invitingly, squeezing my arm. "I know where the cave is. But first, there's something we need to borrow."

"What is it?"

"Just trust me, OK! We're nearly there."

I glanced at him, intrigued, but didn't comment as I concentrated on following the path. We'd just passed the clearing where Zachary usually met up with his friends when the first of the sun's rays peeped over the horizon. A fine mist hovered just above the ground, shrouding the undergrowth in a white haze. Birds chirped every now and then to greet the day, and there was a lovely smell of pine trees and larches in the air.

We walked on in silence for a few minutes before coming to another path that led to a cream-colored cabin. The main door opened as we drew near, and a young man with matted blond hair stepped outside, rubbing still-sleepy eyes. He hopped off the doorstep and threw a set of keys to Zachary, who caught them deftly in midair.

"My folks are still asleep, so please don't start her up till you're on the road."

"Thanks, I owe you," Zachary said, giving his friend a thumbs up to show he understood.

"No problem, and good luck."

He took a long look at me and then went in and closed the door. Zachary headed toward the back of a shed to the side of the cabin, and came back with a four-wheel-drive buggy.

"Come on, then," he said, smiling at my obvious surprise.

"Are we going on that thing?" I asked, hardly believing my eyes.

Zachary's only reply was an even wider smile as he pushed the off-road vehicle up the path.

When we reached the main road, I was confused. I thought this was the road into town, not the way to the little church in the woods where our ill-fated treasure hunt started; that was much farther south.

"Are you sure this is the right way?" I asked anxiously.

"Just trust me!" he replied, climbing onto the buggy.

I hesitated for a moment and then swung my leg over the glossy green paintwork and perched on the seat behind Zachary.

"Ready?" he asked, taking my hands and securing them around his waist.

I nodded shyly, and the vehicle lurched off, catching me unawares. Struggling to keep my balance, I tightened my grip on Zachary and leaned close into his back. With the initial surprise over, I closed my eyes and buried my nose in the warmth of his jacket, free to inhale his delicious lemony smell at my leisure. I wished time could stand still and I could lose myself in that wonderful moment forever, but my mission was too important to succumb to the pleasure.

When I opened my eyes, the forest was scrolling past, its deciduous trees a lush light green and its conifers a lovely stronger green. The road snaked on ahead for a couple of miles before disappearing over the mountain. I had no idea what was on the far side, but I really did have total faith in Zachary.

For the next fifteen minutes, I churned everything around inside my head. With every jolt, I clung a little more closely to Zachary, but all my thoughts were focused on the cave where his father had lived. Yes, that was a good place to start our search. If we looked carefully, we might dig up some clues to help us understand where Jessica was. I even started thinking that, with a little luck, we might actually find my sister there.

Just as I was entertaining this thought, Zachary slowed the buggy to turn onto a track that led off into the woods. My heart dropped uncomfortably in my chest when I recognized the spot where the police had picked us up. My mind was bombarded with images of Mr. Morgan's half-eaten corpse, of the torrential rain, and of me running for my life, which, luckily, had ended in my being saved. Remembering the fear that gripped me when that black form started chasing me, a cold sweat prickled the length of my spine and I couldn't restrain a shudder of retrospective terror. As if he knew what I was thinking, Zachary took one hand off the controls to give my hand a comforting squeeze.

Without a word, we bounced along the track toward the stream that had kept us company for the whole of that fateful day. The previous day's storm had left its mark: every now and then, we saw jagged shapes of fresh pale wood where broken tree trunks were strewn on the ground, and the stream, which had wriggled gleefully down the mountainside only yesterday, was now swollen with excess rainwater. It was so wide that in places I seriously wondered whether we would be able to cross it.

The track was growing narrower and narrower, so we had to slow almost to walking pace. A fallen tree completely blocking our route brought an abrupt end to our little road trip. Resigned to stopping the vehicle, Zachary cut the gas. The sudden silence felt almost eerie, but my ears still thrummed from the sound of the engine, and through this I could make out the rush of the stream and the sound of birdsong.

I stepped off the buggy and went over to the massive pine tree barring the way. Zachary put the keys in his pocket and joined me, his expression unreadable.

"I'm really sorry," he said, having assessed the situation. "Do you think you'll be able to walk?"

I looked at him for a moment before glancing down at my foot. Thanks to the rest and the emergency doctor's care, my ankle was much better.

"No problem," I announced, reminding myself I must keep my foot as straight and level as possible to avoid aggravating the injury.

Zachary climbed over the obstacle blocking the track and took hold of my arm to help me over. For the next ten minutes, we chatted about this and that, trying to avoid any painful or awkward subjects. Then I felt Zachary's hand tense. I looked up anxiously and saw that his face had gone deathly white. I swung around to see what was upsetting him, and saw the area of flattened earth where Mr. Morgan's body had been the day before. There were a few lengths of yellow tape and a lot of footprints to prove that the area had been thoroughly combed for evidence by the police. The surrounding woodland was deserted, having already been searched by the volunteers looking for my sister.

By mutual consent, we decided not to hang around there. I was worried by how pale Zachary was, and I had to admit I couldn't face staying in the place where his father had died a second longer either. We continued on our way, keeping a watchful eye on the rock face on the other side of the stream. The entrance to the tunnel that led to the chamber couldn't be far away now. No more than ten minutes later, the crack in the rock appeared before us.

"I don't believe it!" I cried, realizing how close we'd been to the cabins.

"Oh yes!" Zachary nodded, understanding my surprise. Instead of heading west toward the main river, we had headed north. If we'd carried on following the stream, we'd have been out of the woods on the first day.

The thought of this hurt: we'd been so close to our goal! It seemed clear to me now that Jessica hadn't been as lucky as us, and she hadn't escaped. The volunteers had picked through the whole area without success. I didn't want to contemplate the unthinkable, but it felt obvious that the animal that had attacked Mr. Morgan had also taken my sister. My legs gave way at the thought, and I fell to my knees. The anguish must have been written all over my face because Zachary immediately dropped down beside me, put his arms around me, and whispered words of comfort in my ear. But nothing he said could alleviate my suffering.

I cried silently for some time before finally getting my emotions under control. Eventually I rubbed the back of my hand over my cheeks to dry my tears. Then I stood up and took a deep breath in an effort to pull myself toge-ther.

And that was when I saw it.

Half hidden by the branches of a pine tree, the monster was lurking in the shadows, spying on us. My heart stood still, freezing the blood in my veins. I opened my mouth, but no sound came out. Noticing my strange silence, Zachary looked up and saw the thing too. I felt him tense all over before getting a grip on himself. Without taking his eyes off the monster, he got to his fleet slowly, screening me from the creature with his body.

This movement provoked a low growl from the animal, and I shuddered with terror. The thing stayed hidden a few more seconds and then emerged from the undergrowth into full view. Far too large to be a bear, it was covered in brown hairs from the top of its skull to the tips of its paws. Its forelimbs bore long black claws that looked as sharp as knives. Its face was more like an animal than a human, but there was something strange about it. Impossible as this seemed, the creature's face looked almost as expressive as a human's.

Scrutinizing us with its small black eyes, it stepped closer, quivering its nostrils as if trying to catch our smell. Even though it wasn't behaving particularly aggressively for now, Zachary and I couldn't help shaking with fear. Slowly and infinitely carefully, Zachary reached his hand up to his shoulder where he had slung his rifle. It was a brave move but a reckless one, because it looked like no weapon would get the better of this fur-clad giant looming before us.

The monster suddenly opened its jaws and gave a roar that made us cower in terror and disgust. Its breath was literally not breathable, and I had to make a superhuman effort not to retch.

Zachary was quicker than me to recover. He raised his rifle slowly and released the safety catch before giving a supple twist of his wrist to load it. As if some sixth sense had warned the animal of the danger, it leapt toward us and launched itself into the air. I just managed to avoid it by jumping aside, but Zachary wasn't so lucky. Dropping his rifle, he bellowed and held his arms out to try to counter the monster's sudden attack.

When I saw Zachary grappling with that beast, my instincts got the upper hand over my reason, which had stopped functioning altogether. Without even thinking what I was doing, I grabbed the rifle and aimed at the animal. As if I'd rehearsed this a thousand times, my hands settled into position on the polished wood and, without the slightest hesitation, my finger squeezed the trigger. The shot fired, kicking me backward violently. To my surprise, I hit the animal and it gave a great yowl of pain before running off into the forest.

18
Revelations

It took me several minutes to analyze what had just happened. I, Madison Greenwood, had frightened off a monster twice my own height. With my head still ringing from the gunshot, I was standing staring vacantly at the rifle when I heard Zachary move and give a moan beside me. I threw down the rifle as if it had bitten me, and knelt beside his prostrate body. The left leg of his pants was covered in blood and his sweater was badly torn.

"Are you OK?" I asked, running my hands anxiously over his battered body.

His only reply was a groan of agony when I touched a particularly painful spot.

"Ouch! Be careful, please!"

"I'm sorry. I'm just trying to see how badly you're hurt."

Zachary struggled to sit up, still dazed from the animal's onslaught.

"It feels like he bit my leg, but, apart from that, I think I'm OK."

"I think it's more like he scratched you with his claws," I said, examining the parallel lines pierced through his jeans.

"What do you think it was?" he asked, grimacing.

"I have no idea. Some kind of bear, maybe."

"There's a first-aid kit in my backpack," he said with a sigh.

He was clearly finding it difficult to slip the strap off his shoulder, so I helped him, and opened the backpack. I took out a water bottle and handed it to him. He opened it gratefully and gulped back the water while I looked for the first-aid kit. After a few minutes, I finally found a small gray pouch with a red cross embroidered on the front. I opened the zipper and found a pair of scissors; then I tried to make light of the situation, brandishing them in Zachary's face.

"You'll have to take off your jeans if you don't want me to cut them up in little bits," I threatened playfully, snapping the blades together.

"Are you kidding? There's no way I can."

I brought the scissors up to the seam of his jeans, sneakily savoring a moment's revenge for all those times he'd treated me to his sardonic sneers.

"OK!" he cried, stopping my hand where it was. "But I'll need some help."

"It will be my pleasure," I beamed.

Zachary's face contorted in pain as he wriggled to slip off his jeans. I did my best to help him, and this delicate operation brought a guilty flush to my cheeks. The flush only deepened when I saw his shorts and his bare legs, but all embarrassment was brushed aside once I could see the row of oozing slashes over his left thigh. The beast had left its mark, and I was pretty sure Zachary would bear the scars forever.

I opened up the first-aid kit again to look for disinfectant and bandages. When I found a bottle of antiseptic, I showed it to Zachary apologetically. He closed his eyes and gritted his teeth as I poured the solution over his wounds. He sat up and tensed his muscles several times, but didn't cry out in pain once. Next I put some ointment on the wounds before wrapping his leg firmly in a bandage. Then I helped him take off his sweater, and I cleaned up the gashes over his back. He let me do this without a sound, but when I'd finished my work and he could put his clothes back on, his forehead was covered in sweat.

I put everything away in the backpack and sat back on my heels to consider our situation. We were in serious trouble¬¬—starting with the fact that, even with my help, Zachary wouldn't be able to walk very far. But that was peanuts compared to the threat of the animal coming back at any minute. And now that it was injured, it wasn't going to be in the sunniest of moods.

The thought of it made me puff out my cheeks as I blew out a long, deep breath, and I stood up to have a look at the entrance to the cave in the rock face on the far side of the stream. An idea was starting to form inside my head. Maybe if we could cross the stream, we would be able to shelter inside the cave. But we still had to consider the fact that the animal could then trap us inside.

"The emergency services are bound to come soon," Zachary said wearily, interrupting my thoughts. "When I left, my mom was still at the hospital with Emily, but I left her a voicemail to tell her we were coming here."

"That was a good idea, but in the meantime, we need to find somewhere to hide just in case that bear thing comes back. Do you think you could get over to the cave there?"

"You're kidding, right? The water's so high, we'd get totally soaked. And it's not warm today anyway."

"If we took off our pants and sneakers, it should be OK…"

The corners of Zachary's mouth suddenly curled into a smile. Blushing furiously, I looked away and busied myself untying my sneakers.

Despite the fact that Zachary kept eyeing me up and down, the crossing was much easier than I'd anticipated.

After helping Zachary across, I did several return trips to collect firewood. We'd agreed we should stay in the mouth of the cave and light a fire, believing that was the best way to guarantee our safety. The thing was an animal after all, and animals are afraid of fire; everyone knows that. We both hoped the fire would be enough to keep it away.

Once I was satisfied that the fire was big and strong enough, I relaxed a little and stood warming my bare legs. Then I slipped my jeans and sneakers back on, aware of Zachary's eyes avidly watching my every move. It took all my concentration just to tie my laces.

"So…" he said in a velvety voice. "What do we do now?"

The tone of his voice was so loaded with innuendo that I felt a shiver run through me. I didn't know what he had in mind, but the way he'd said those words had set my imagination racing.

"I could look for clues in the cave while you stay here," I suggested, feeling this was a sensible idea.

"You'll have plenty of time to do that when the emergency services get here," he retorted. "And you can't leave me on my own; I might go into shock. In fact, I'm real cold right now…"

The sensuous drawl in his voice as he said this made me raise an eyebrow. There was every possibility the animal's attack on him could have repercussions, but his sneaky smile didn't quite match his words. I hesitated for a while and then decided I couldn't take the risk, so I walked over slowly and sat down right next to him.

His smile broadened noticeably as he leaned against me and closed his eyes contentedly. I could feel the warmth radiating from his body, and mine reacted involuntarily, shivering despite the blazing heat flowing through my veins. What little sense I had left evaporated when he took me in his arms. His face was so close to mine that I could feel his warm breath against my neck. The longing in his eyes broke down the last of my resistance. I brought my mouth up to his and kissed him, just brushing over his lips at first, and then with real passion.

Zachary responded to my kiss with an ardor that matched my own. His hands were hesitant for a moment but soon they ventured to increasingly intimate parts of my body, making me moan with pleasure. Not wanting to be outdone, though, I slipped his sweater off so that I could stroke his back. When he fumbled awkwardly with the clasp on my bra, I gave an impatient sigh and undid the recalcitrant thing myself. I shuddered at the feel of his warm hand over my naked skin, although he was barely touching me. After a brief hesitation, he took my breast in his hand and started gently teasing my nipple. That was enough to make me lose all self-control.

I knew I was playing a dangerous game, but there was no one here this time to cry out and stop me in my tracks. Our pants soon joined the rest of our clothes on the ground, and we ended up lying next to each other, skin to skin. I let my hands travel over his body, every now and then touching his erection, but I had one last flash of clear-headedness when my hand unexpectedly came in contact with the bandage on his thigh.

"Isn't it hurting?" I asked very quietly, drawing back slightly.

"No," he breathed, but I'm sure he was lying.

We lay there motionless for a while, breathless and gazing at each other with feverish eyes.

"Are you sure?" Zachary asked, suddenly losing confidence.

With everything that had happened the day before, I was no longer sure of anything. But the fact that I'd lost my sister and we'd come close to death more than once had swept away the last vestiges of the moralizing young lady I had always been.

"Yes," I whispered, kissing him again.

The fire running through my veins blazed all the more ardently when I felt his erection throbbing against my stomach. I moaned with pleasure and pressed myself closer to him. He turned me onto my back and lay gently on top of me, staring into my eyes, which were swimming with desire. Zachary was trembling in every limb, and I felt his penis probing at the opening to my most intimate part. I closed my eyes and prepared to cope with the pain of my hymen tearing. But nothing happened. Zachary's virility had suddenly evaporated. What had stood magnificent and proud only moments before now hung limply between his thighs. What was going on? What did I do wrong?

I was still a virgin, of course, but I read a lot and there had been times when I'd chanced across really steamy passages that left little to the imagination. So I was pretty sure I hadn't done anything that could produce this sort of result. In fact, I felt I'd been on the bold side considering it was my first time. Something about my body, maybe? The intense way boys usually looked at me made it clear that my figure was acceptable in every way, but Zachary's reaction was enough to start a complex.

With my heart thumping uncomfortably, I gently pushed Zachary off, sat up, and put my clothes back on. I snuck a look at him before moving closer to the fire, and I started poking it with a piece of wood just to have something to do. I really didn't know what to say. I felt so humiliated that treacherous tears threatened to roll down my cheeks at any minute. Out of the corner of my eye, I could see that Zachary had put his pants on and was leaning against the rock face, looking mortified.

"I'm so sorry," he managed after several minutes of embarrassed silence.

It was very obvious that those simple words had taken a superhuman effort to pronounce. But I had no idea how to reply. I didn't know which of us most needed comforting. Because I wasn't responding at all, he spoke again, and there was a sort of anger in his voice that start-led me.

"It's not your fault," he blurted. "I'm the one with the problem. Anyway, you're way better off without a guy like me."

That statement, pronounced even more curtly than what had gone before, cut through the silence like a sentence in a court of law. My heart was already so wounded from the events of the last couple of days that it shattered into a thousand pieces. A fact that had weirdly escaped my notice until now suddenly struck me: I realized I was desperately in love with Zachary. This revelation ached so much I had to close my eyes to contain the flow of tears ready to spill down my face.

A heartfelt curse made me look up. Zachary was staring at me with so much pain on his face that it took all my strength to stop myself running over to take refuge in his arms. Then a flash of anger blazed through his eyes, and it was only then that I understood the full implication of what had just happened: Emily was not the only one who had been abused by her father. Zachary had been too.

19
A Big Surprise

For a moment, I didn't say anything, stunned by what I had just learned. Then I stood up and slowly went over to where he was sitting.

"I think I know what happened to you," I said softly, wiping the tear marks from my face. "And I understand why you never told anyone. But now that your father's… no longer here, you could maybe ask for some help. There's a psychologist at high school and—"

"It's none of your business!" he snapped, looking up and glowering at me fiercely.

"Oh yes it is my business!" I retorted, dropping to my knees beside him.

I grabbed a hold of his black hair with one hand and put my lips to his. Zachary recoiled and tried to push me away, but I'd really made up my mind because I knew that the future of our relationship depended on that kiss.

He struggled for a few seconds, but I held out and felt his resistance weaken. Eventually he gave in and his mouth grew softer. I could feel him shaking as he took me in his arms, and he kissed me with a passion that was tinged with both anger and gentleness, making me completely melt. But I felt intuitively that if I gave myself now I could easily ruin my chances of building something lasting with him. I drew away from his kiss with some regret and looked deep into his green eyes, which were filled with despair.

"I love you," I confided seriously, "and I can wait."

I gave him a moment to gather his emotions, but he didn't say anything. I stood with a quiet sigh and started walking away in the hopes that I could hide my tears of disappointment. For a few minutes, I'd thought we might be able to…

"Maddie," he called behind me, instantly halting my retreat.

But I'll never know what he wanted to say, because at the exact moment he said my name, we heard a vehicle backfire somewhere outside the tunnel. Help was on its way.

Rather unwillingly, I left Zachary's side and walked around the fire out into the sunshine. Two all-terrain vehicles came to a stop right in front of me.

"What the hell are you doing here?" a man practically yelled, and I recognized the same police officer from the day before. "Couldn't you stay home like a good girl?"

My tears brought a stop to his robust reprisals.

"What's happened? Did you find something?"

"No, no," I replied, wiping my cheeks for the ump-teenth time.

I couldn't see how I would explain what I'd just been through with Zachary so I defaulted back to the first thing that came into my head.

"We were attacked by a kind of bear thing," I said, "and Zachary's injured."

I pointed to the mouth of the tunnel, and the police officer climbed swiftly down from his vehicle and ran inside to see Zachary. The second officer jumped to the ground too and followed him into the cave.

This moment alone was exactly what I needed, because I still wasn't confident I could suppress my feelings. I felt sure Zachary wouldn't talk about the abuse, and I understood his reasons. There were likely to be far-reaching implications for the rest of his family if he decided to speak out. But that decision rang the death knell for any future relationship between us, because I just couldn't see how we would cope without help.

I heaved yet another sigh and looked out across the forest; it looked a lot less dangerous now that help was at hand. Sure, the animal was big and strong, but it surely couldn't stand up to two armed officers.

A noise behind me made me turn around. Zachary was limping painfully out of the tunnel, supported by the officers. He managed to make it over to the first vehicle, and the officer helped him in. The other officer put out the fire before helping me into his passenger seat.

When we finally set off, Zachary turned to look at me, and there was a determination in his eye that made my heart give an optimistic skip. He seemed to mutter something to me, but I couldn't hear a thing over the sound of the engines. All the same, a spark of hope flickered through me because I felt fairly confident I'd lip read the words he'd just said. Words that opened the doors wide to hopes of a future for us. And those words were: "I love you!"

My face glowing with happiness, I thoroughly enjoyed our trip back to safety. The sunshine was glorious and the green woodland spectacular while my heart floated as if on butterfly wings. But the smile fell from my face all too quickly when I saw there was another patrol car parked outside my family's cabin. My chest felt heavy with dread when I heard the police officer who was driving me mutter, "What's going on here? No one's told me..."

I leapt out of the vehicle before it even stopped. As far as I could see, the only thing that could possibly have happened was that Jessica's body had been found. I didn't know I had any tears left, but my cheeks were wet yet again at the thought of how devastated my parents must be. I'd been stupid to try looking for my sister myself. Selfishly focusing on my own feelings of guilt, I'd failed to consider how my parents would react when they found I'd gone.

Blinded by tears, I ran over to the steps and bounded up them in record time. I strode across the terrace and through the door to the kitchen before stopping in my tracks. Sitting comfortably cradling a mug of hot chocolate, my sister was describing her adventures, her cheeks flushed with excitement.

I stood idiotically with my arms hanging limply by my side for several seconds.

"Maddie!" Jessica cried, leaping up from her chair. "Where did you go?"

My parents stood up and came over to put their arms around me, making me break down in irresistible sobs. We clung to each other for many minutes, laughing, crying, and relieved to be together again. Then we went and sat down at the table so that the police officer who had watched us in discreet silence could carry on taking Jessica's statement. I couldn't wait to hear her story, so I asked if she could start at the beginning again. Jessica glanced at the officer, who nodded his consent.

"What happened to you? Did that man hurt you?" I asked anxiously.

"No," she said simply. "He dragged me through the woods for a few minutes before I built up the courage to bite his hand. That made him drop his knife, and I managed to jab him under the chin with my elbow. Then I ran as fast as I could, and he couldn't catch me. The only problem was, I was lost."

My incredulity and admiration must have been written all over my face, because she savored the moment by taking a long, slow sip of hot chocolate before continuing.

"I walked through the woods for maybe an hour, and it was starting to get really dark and I couldn't see a thing. Except somewhere up ahead, I could see someone had made a fire. I went over cautiously, and I could see a couple camping."

"So what did you do?" I asked, finding it hard to believe how lucky she'd been.

"Well, I just told them I was lost. They both laughed because it turns out they were lost too," she said, smiling at the memory.

"That's incredible! And how did you find your way home?"

"First we spent the night in their tent, and they let me share their sleeping bag. Then we walked all day until I suddenly remembered something I learned at my holiday camp last year."

"And what was that?" asked my father, who hadn't said a word till that point.

"The fact that moss always grows on the northern side at the foot of a tree. So we headed west and we ended up running into the volunteer group who were looking for me."

Having finished her story, she took another gulp of her drink with a smile playing on her lips. My dad squeezed my mom's hand while she wiped a few stray tears from her cheeks. The police officer closed his notebook, ready to get up and leave us together.

I sat there looking at my family, not sure what the future held in store for me. But one thing was sure: it seemed full of promise.

20
Back at the Cave

A dark shape moved about in the shadows, lit only by the feeble glow coming through the gap in the rock. The sun would soon set, and the animal was using the last of the light to rummage through the abandoned clothes in search of a scent that would send it out to hunt again.

It pushed aside a bag and noticed a scrap of white fabric dirty with dust. It reached out a forelimb to pick the thing up, but withdrew at the last minute with a groan of pain. It turned to look at its shoulder, where warm blood was seeping through its lustrous brown fur. There was a small hole in the skin, harboring the bullet that had been tormenting the animal for nearly two whole days.

Ignoring the throbbing pain, the creature gritted its teeth and closed its eyes, angling its long black claws toward the wound with great determination. With another groan of agony, it poked at the wound for several seconds before gasping in surprise when it found the bullet. Extricating the bullet from the wound, the animal brought this strange object close to its eyes to inspect it. The blood-smeared cylindrical piece of metal gleamed softly in the darkness.

The monster roared angrily and turned its attention back to the scrap of white fabric. It wrinkled its nose, recognizing a smell it had met before: the smell of a little girl sweating in terror. A smell that provoked a mood of revenge.

As the animal clutched that small piece of cotton, a strange smile teased the corners of its mouth in its near-human face. Then it threw back its head and howled triumphantly before turning and heading back along the tunnel toward the forest.

To be continued…